AVIATION

THE SKY PILOT'S GREAT CHASE

OR

Jack Ralston's Dead Stick Landing

BY

AMBROSE NEWCOMB

Author of "The Sky Detectives," "Eagles of the Sky," "Wings Over the Rockies," etc.

Published by

THE GOLDSMITH PUBLISHING CO.

NEW YORK   CHICAGO

CONTENTS

CONTENTS

The Sky Pilot's Great Chase

CHAPTER I

THE CLANG OF THE FIRE BELL

"Well, I kinder guess now this here little ol' ho-tel in Salt Lake City 's got our experience in Cheyenne knocked all to flinders. Good room, twin beds that keep you from hoggin' all the covers on a cool night an' as to *eats,* say it's sure prime stuff, though mebbe I ain't no judge 'long any line 'cept quantity. How 'bout it, Jack, ol' hoss?"

The happy-go-lucky speaker was an old friend of ours, one Perk, and the companion to whom he addressed his question was his bosom pal, Jack Ralston of the U. S. Secret Service. Nevertheless, it seemed that Perk was now known as Gabe Smith, a woods guide of wide experience who in the course of his wanderings had managed to pick up a smattering of aviation, a particularly useful thing in these air-minded days.

And Jack, whenever there was a third party

within hearing, was always referred to as Mr. John Jacob Astorbilt, a wideawake young millionaire sportsman always seeking novel thrills hunting big game by means of the latest type airship.

All this had a good and sufficient reason back of it, which will be placed before the reader ere we have gone deeply into this log covering the latest undertaking of the two redoubtable sky detectives.

"Oh! things suit me okay, Perk," was Jack's rather indifferent reply, as he smiled at his companion's grinning, enthusiastic face. "Somehow I don't seem to set quite as much store by my meals as you do but I'll say the food is pretty decent—better than the restaurant stuff we used to eat three times a day over in old Cheyenne."

"Hot ziggety dog! I should say so. But what tickles me most of all, partner, is the dandy ship Uncle Sam turned over to us after we climbed out o' all that hot stuff down on the west coast o' Florida. She's a genuine cloud-chaser, boy, an' don't take any guy's dust—am I right 'bout that, Boss?"

"I'll admit she's a prize boat and no mistake. Able to drop down on land or water and with skis in place could do the same on a frozen lake or the deepest snow the Northland ever saw. Yes, it would be hard to beat our ship, Perk."

"Right up to date she is. Look at the shiny aluminum pontoons an' rubber tired wheels peekin' out from the bow ends. The Hamilton propeller that does its stuff to the dot; a real Hasler Telmot Flight Meter; aluminum oil tanks so light and yet so strong; earth-inducter compass next to infallible; Eclipse Starter—gosh amighty, if there's a single thing worth its salt that our ship ain't got I'd like to hear 'bout it."

Jack laughed. He had a whole-souled laugh that did any one good just to hear it—kind of gave you a warm feeling and seemed to draw you into friendly relations with the clear-eyed young aviator.

"Just one thing lacking, partner, in the round-up if you stop to think of it. We felt the need of it on our last jaunt* when in the midst of the most dreadful fog-belt either of us had ever struck, we climbed to a ten thousand foot ceiling only to have ice begin to form on our wings. Haven't forgotten that, eh, Perk old fellow?"

"Ginger pop an' the weasel! I guess now I ain't. You've crabbed my game, buddy, that's what you've done. But as we ain't, so far, been sent to the South Pole to help get an explorer out o' his bad fix in the ice, I kinder guess we don't need that ice meltin' device much. Got to draw

*See *Wings Over the Rockies.*

a line somewhere you know, Boss, else the ship'll be so loaded down with new contraptions there won't be any storage room for the grub-pile!"

"And sure enough that's where the shoe would pinch, Perk. Grub, and plenty of it is the real necessity to have aboard. It bobs up just three times a day right along and with mighty long waits between according to your way of looking at it."

"You said it, partner! I've tried goin' shy on the eats but it don't seem to work worth a red cent. Right away there's a mutiny breaks out under the midship hatch an' I jest *got* to surrender. But, to change the subject, I'm botherin' my poor brain tryin' to figger out which way we'll face when the orders come breezin' along?"

Jack chuckled as he lolled back in his comfortable easy-chair for they chanced to be sitting in their third-floor hotel room while engaging in this little confab.

"It's a toss-up I'd say, Perk," he remarked a bit mysteriously. You know the whole wide world is our hunting ground as you've so often boasted. International crooks breed a like species of detectives. When they take to flying, the Secret Service has to go them one better. Our familiarity with airships helped to rustle this job for us and we've got to make good, no matter whether we fly to Japan, India, South Africa or any other old country under the sun."

Perk displayed the proper amount of enthusiasm as this wide subject came along, for his eyes sparkled, and he grinned broadly.

"You bet, Jack ol' hoss," he blurted out, "an' like's not the slick way we put through that last deal down on the west Florida coast, fetchin' the king o' booze smugglers back with us to the bar o' justice has made us solid with the Head at Washington."*

"I shouldn't wonder buddy," was all Jack said, not being given to blowing his own horn as Perk often did, being only human as he would explain, and knowing a good thing when he saw it.

"We dropped in at this 'ere airport," Perk continued, "'cordin' to orders a hull week back, sailin' under new names to hide our identities an' here we be, killin' time an' waitin' to make a bee line for any place that happens to be in need o' cleanin' up. We're the boss outfit for that sorter job, on'y I'd give a heap to know what's what."

"That's a weakness of yours, Perk. Now in my case it doesn't give me one minute's uneasiness. Whether I'm working in Paris, Cairo or Timbuktu makes no difference, I calculate on get-

*See *Eagles of the Sky.*

ting enough to eat, pick up plenty of sleep and beat the game if its possible. Nothing else will satisfy me, as you pretty well know, brother."

"When I happen to wake up in the small hours o' the night, Jack, I just get bothered 'bout the next layout and sometimes wonder if I'm right then an' there across the Pacific or playin' a swift game down in Nicaragua f'r instance. Feels a whole lot like we might be reg'lar gypsies, changin' our camp every night."

"Well, what of it?" demanded Jack, looking vastly amused. "It wouldn't be the first time that name was applied to me for you remember when I first broke into this game it was as a gypsy pilot, doing stunts with my 'chute at county fairs and Harvest Homes all around the country. That name always did sound kind of sweet in my ears. I like it to this day, in fact."

"Mebbe now, it might be that you could give a sorter guess 'bout that job we're goin' to have tacked on to us right away? How 'bout it, old hoss?"

"Oh! that doesn't concern me one whit, Perk. Just hold your horses and take things as they come. There's a bit of fun being kept in the dark about these affairs. Makes me think of the times we used to have grab-bags at church fairs, when you paid a penny or a nickel and pulled out something queer. Say, didn't we feel a great big thrill just before making the grab? Take things easy and let the folks at Headquarters do most of the worrying. That's what I call logic, buddy."

"Huh! mebbe so," grunted Perk, eyeing his comrade quizically as though more than half suspecting that if Jack chose, at least he could give a fairly good guess covering their next thrilling assignment. "But that sorter philosophy don't cut any figger when I lie awake nights cudgelin' my slow-workin' brains an' tryin' to get the answer. But then, like as not, we ain't goin' to stick to this queer old burg much longer an' I sure do hope the wire givin' us full directions in cipher comes along right soon."

Jack Ralston, as the readers of the three preceding stories in this series of Sky Detective adventures already know, had been building up quite an enviable reputation in the Secret Service of the Government, being entrusted with a number of the most important tasks that were cropping up from time to time.

These necessitated not only a cool head, quick decisions and plenty of nerve, but also demanded a thorough knowledge of aeronautics, since many malfactors in these very modern days were taking to the air in order to facilitate their unlawful operations so that it had become necessary to meet them on their own grounds and go them one better.

His best pal was Gabe Perkiser, whose odd name was usually shortened to Perk. He was fully ten years older than Jack and at the time our country entered the World War chanced to be connected with the balloon corps so that for some time he found himself a manipulator of an observation balloon, better known as a "sausage."

Tiring of this monotonous life, the active Perk took up aviation. Here he was in his element and few there were during those mad months when the American army was breaking the Hindenberg line and pushing through the terrible thickets and machine-gun nests of the Argonne, who attained a higher rating as a fearless pilot than Gabe Perkiser.

He had numerous glorious victories to his credit, having sent down many enemy flyers in blazing coffins but eventually met with a serious mishap that sent him to a field hospital and kept him out of the rest of that frightful campaign.

Recovering in due time, Perk had come back to the States bent on securing some sort of employment that would give him all the excitement his system demanded. This he found when he joined the Northwest Mounted Police of Canada. The fact that one of his parents had been born across the line while the other was a

Maine Yankee, gave Perk the opening he desired and his yearning for adventure after that was never left unsatisfied.

But after a while he even began to tire of such a lonely life as his duties entailed and floated down once more to the country of his birth. There by some happy accident Jack ran across him and recognizing a kindred spirit, he induced Perk to apply for a position in the Secret Service.

Still later, when he had been detailed to make use of his ability as an air pilot to carry on with a certain job that had been placed in his hands, Jack remembered Perk. It was essential that he have an assistant aboard his ship and so he negotiated matters so that Perk was ordered to report to him and act as co-pilot for an indefinite length of time, an arrangement that gave both the greatest satisfaction possible.

They were after all a well matched pair. What one lacked the other possessed in abundance. Jack was able to hold his more impulsive comrade in check when safety first became their watchword, and on the other hand when a show of dash and vigor was the order of the day, Perk was apt to take the lead and strike terror in the hearts of the enemy.

Naturally enough inaction became irksome to Perk and he fretted because he loathed remaining quiet when his whole system was calling for accomplishing things.

Jack, of course, was the one who laid out the plan of campaign, he being much better fitted for such essential matters. Perk on the other hand really needed some one above to give him the order and check his impulsiveness on accasion. So they got on together admirably, and worked like a well matched team.

To be sure Jack sometimes knew a bit more than he chose to tell Perk but he always had good and sufficient reasons for holding back such information and his lack of knowledge, until such time as his leader saw fit to take him wholly into his confidence, did Perk no harm whatever.

It did, however, cause him to lie awake nights wondering and speculating as to what would be next on the program. He would try his best to tempt Jack to commit himself but all to no purpose, for the other put him off with one plea or another with Perk returning to the attack time and again.

They had had their wonderfully efficient plane lodged in a hangar out at the flying field where just so often each day an air-mail pilot was scheduled to arrive or depart with the letter sacks of the Post Office Department. This courtesy had been bestowed upon them by a Mr. Spencer Gibbons a private flyer and a man of considerable means who came and went as his fancy dictated.

He had met Jack while the latter, under strict injunctions from the Department, was posing as a young and enthusiastic air-minded millionaire and had given him the use of the single-ship hangar while he, Gibbons, was off on a jaunt that took him down to the Mexican border, but as he was expected back at any time now they had changed the location of their amphibian that same afternoon.   It now rested secure in another nearby hangar that happened to be empty and which Jack could hire, being liberally supplied with funds by his generous employer, Uncle Sam.

This was only a minor incident, and yet it was fated to play an important part in the general network of things, and hence to be the cause of many speculations on the part of the two chums.

Perk, acting under the direction of his mate, had taken a vast amount of pleasure in loading up a supply of commodities. These consisted of the ordinary supplies, such as an old and experienced camper would be apt to put down on his list and possibly a few special dainties that particularly appealed to Perk's appetite and which he meant to spring upon his fellow flyer at some convenient time when both of them happened to be ravenously hungry and there came a chance to build a cooking fire.

Then too, it was always their day by day plan to keep a full stock of fuel and lubricating oil aboard their boat since there never would be much warning given them when the order to hop-off came by telegraph.

They seldom allowed a favorable flying day to pass by without going aloft in order to keep in practice and also be certain the precious ship was in first class condition for immediate service. As they had not had possession of the wonder plane for any great length of time, Jack was always finding out some fresh discovery calculated to increase his admiration for his craft and evoke a volley of expressions from the voluble Perk.

The sun had already set and dusk was begin ning to gather, telling them it was about time to descend to the dining room and partake of their customary evening meal. After that Perk would doubtless wander around to the nearest moving-picture palace and allow his feverish soul to have full swing in the excitement depicted on the silver screen.

Just then there came along one of those little incidents that sometimes turn out to have un-suspected potentialities. Perk seemed to catch it first, for he jumped up and broke loose by cry-ing:

"Hear that, partner? The fire alarm as sure as you're born and me, always like a little kid, crazy to run with the engine and watch the fire boys go through with their thrillin' stunts. Come along, buddy—supper c'n wait a bit for us an' we'll be all the hungrier at that. Snatch up your hat an' let's go!"

CHAPTER II

TRAPPED BY THE FLAMES

Jack seemed perfectly willing to accompany his chum, even if it did put a damper on their supper. Possibly he was like the vast majority of American youngsters in his youth, and could never resist the lure of a fire.

Accordingly they hurried down to the lower floor and dashed outside.

"Which way now, partner?" gasped Perk who was a bit short of wind after making that rush downstairs, not waiting to use the clevator. "I don't see any glow in the sky to tell where the blaze c'n be."

"Follow the crowd—that's our only cue, Perk," Jack hastened to say. "Listen to all that row—must be a fire engine heading to the spot; ought to set us right, I reckon."

"Sure thing, Boss an' here she comes a rushin' along like an express train—no hosses though, these days which knocks a whole lot o' the picture silly. On your way, John Jacob, I'm with you!"

They ran like deer, side by side. Others were

streaming ahead, everybody displaying the utmost zeal to get to the fire before the conflagration was smothered by the streams of water turned on it.

Perk was in his glory—this sort of thing appealed to his nature as a pond would to a flock of thirsty ducks. Only for his lack of wind he might have indulged in a few cowboy whoops as he tore up one street and down another, touching elbows with his pard and eagerly straining his eyes in the hope of presently detecting a gust of smoke that would proclaim their arrival at the scene of operations.

"Thar she blows!" Perk suddenly gasped, "see that black smudge blowin' in from a side street ol' hoss? Jest one more burst an' we'll be Johnny on the spot! Wow! ain't this glorious sport though?"

Jack made no answer, since there was nothing to say and he needed all his breath to keep going, not yet having caught his second wind.

Already a large crowd had gathered and was milling this way and that, trying in every way possible to catch a better view of the house that was the object of all these activities. Several engines had arrived and were making a great noise as they began to throw streams of water on the imperiled building as well as its near neighbors that would soon be in danger should the fire get a better start.

"Whee! smoke aplenty but so far I don't lamp any fire," Perk was saying in disjointed fragments as he and Jack stopped running and commenced to make their way through gaps in the moving crowds.

"A four-story frame building," observed Jack as though that fact gripped his attention first of all, "and looks like it might be a tenement in the bargain."

"I kinder guess you're 'bout right there, partner." Perk chimed in. "See the women and kids huddled up over yonder, some o' 'em holdin' bundles o' stuff they've grabbed up when they hurried to get out! Ain't that too bad, though —the poor things, to git burned out o' their homes."

It was a picture well calculated to wring the heart of a softy like Perk. Apparently all of the tenants had managed to get clear of the smoke-filled halls for the police officers standing guard at the exit were preventing any of the wildly excited women from rushing back into the building, doubtless with the intention of saving some beloved article which had a value in their eyes far in excess of its intrinsic one. Although they fought desperately to push past, the stern guardians of the law stood between and held them back, as if acting under the belief that such an act would be sheer suicide with all that dense smoke filling the halls and stairways.

"There, I saw a flash of flame jest then, Jack!" suddenly ejaculated Perk and if there was a little tinge of satisfaction in his voice it was hardly to be wondered at, the old boyish spirit rising up superior to his feeling of sympathy for the unfortunate families thus dispossessed of their humble homes.

Jack himself had noted the fact, although he made no remark, only shook his head sadly as if recognizing the fact that despite the fight put up by the fire laddies the frame building was very likely doomed.

They stood there and watched operations for some little time meanwhile other engines had come up, attached their hose to convenient hydrants and added fresh streams to those already drenching the buildings.

"Hot ziggetty dog! this here is gettin' some monotonous, partner," Perk finally remarked, "mebbe after all we'd show good sense by hikin' back to the hotel and tacklin' that grub."

"Don't be in such a big hurry, buddy," objected the other who usually did prove to be some sticker, as Perk often observed, "since we've gone and made the run we ought to see a bit more of the fire. Supper will keep and besides, you're likely to have a bigger vacuum to be filled. What say to taking a turn around and getting a view from another quarter?"

"That ain't a bad idea boy, let's get a move on," agreed Perk who always liked a change of base when it promised further novelty.

"Come this way then," Jack told him, starting to the left, "the crowd thins out off yonder, and we'll be able to push through much easier. They still keep on coming though; men, women and lots of children wo'd be better off at home I reckon still, what would you have? Chances are the average kid is just as wild to run with the fire engine as when we went into action!"

"Seems like it," chuckled Perk, grinning amiably at a bunch of half-grown lads who had just come up and were staring goggle-eyed at the red streaks of leaping fire that appeared frequently amidst all the dense smoke.

Jack had been right in choosing to take the left turn, for they presently had everything to themselves. Evidently the other side of the building presented the most picturesque part of the conflagration, for hardly a straggler was met as they pursued their way.

"Here's the rear of the tenement," Jack remarked in a loud voice for the assembled steamers were kicking up so much noise that it was not easy to make himself heard. "See, they're trying to wet down the building that backs up so close to the one that's afire. It's a four-story one at that and luckily built of brick, which may save it from catching fire."

There seemed to be a rear entrance for a cop was standing guard there, apparently to keep any frantic tenant from rushing inside in the mad hope of rescuing some cherished object that had been forgotten in the frantic dash from the building earlier in the evening.

Flames were now coming out of several windows in the upper part of the doomed structure. On seeing this Jack lost all hope of the house being saved through the heroic efforts of the striving firemen.

"It's bound to go, Perk," he remarked, "I'm sorry for those poor families that stand to lose everything they've got in the wide world. Such as they never have a red cent of fire insurance. Look at that burst of flame will you? Small chance anybody'd have if they were unfortunate enough to get trapped up there!"

"Ugh! don't mention it, partner!" cried the shocked Perk, his gaze fixed on the red tongues that kept flickering out of the upper windows like angry demons. "Many a time I've dreamed I was in a fire-trap like this here, an' had to slide down the waterpipe with greedy fingers like them flames up there settin' my clothes afire, singein' my hair and eyebrows an' nigh chokin' me in the bargain. I'll dream o' this for a month o' Sundays but ain't it a thrillin' sight though?"

That was just like honest-hearted Perk—filled with pity for those who stood to lose all their scanty earthly possessions, yet fascinated and duly thrilled by the fire itself and the whole surrounding panorama.

A minute afterwards Perk burst out in most intense excitement, gripping his chum's arm with a strained clutch as he cried:

"Je-ru-sa-lem crickets! now ain't that a danged shame though?"

"What do you mean buddy?" demanded Jack, also thrilled.

"Up yonder at that third-story window where the smoke's comin' out in big whoops—I certain sure did see a poor woman reach out, wringin' her hands like she was hopin' they started to set the ladders up—then she fell back again in the smoke—oh! Jack, she's goin' to be smothered an' burned to a crisp if nobody c'n get to her in time!"

CHAPTER III

BRIDGING THE GAP

"Which window, Perk?" cried the startled Jack, staring upward.

"That one—third from the further end—gee whiz! like I might be in a cutout—brain all in a mixup—what c'n we do, Boss—knock that cop over an' skoot upstairs?"

"Not any of that stuff, buddy," Jack told the impulsive one in his impressive fashion. "He represents the Law, and so do we. Besides, look at the smoke rolling out of that rear door, it would be the last of us if we started that fool racket."

"But—somethin's *got* to be done, Jack — we jest can't stand here and let a poor woman be burned to death. Do somethin' partner, 'cause I'm flyin' blind in a messy fog and can't see where I ought to head."

His voice and manner were both imploring, and Jack could not but be impressed by the gravity of the occasion.

"Sure you saw some one are you, Perk?" he demanded.

"Jack, I got good eyesight, an'—looky there, right now, she's back at the same window an' *will* you b'lieve me if she ain't got a kid alongside her? Wouldn't that jar you, ol' hoss?"

Jack no longer entertained any doubt regarding the truth of what his comrade had seen for he too could dimly make out moving figures at the third window from the end of the burning tenement.

"They're makin' motions to us right now!" sang out the greatly distressed Perk in new agony of mind. "I swan if I don't think they're meanin' to make the jump an' it'd be a crack-up dead sure!"

Startled by his own works Perk began to make violent gestures, as though endeavoring to warn the frightened woman not to dream of jumping.

"Hold your hosses—we'll get goin' an' have you out o' that mess in a jiffy;" and then turning upon his companion Perk almost savagely demanded: "It's up to us, Jack—now how're we goin' to do it?"

"There's only one chance that I can see," Jack told him, "which is by way of this other building here. We must rush up to the third floor and if luck backs us we can find some way of passing over to her room—see, it's only a matter of five or six feet at most. Come on, buddy!"

"Whoop! here we go then!" thundered Perk,

making one more sweep of his arms as if to reassure the trapped inmate of the tenement and then rushing in the wake of the fast moving Jack.

Several people were emerging from a rear door of the brick building, and lugging all manner of household things in a mad endeavor to save cherished possessions. Evidently they had been seized by an overpowering fear that the fire might leap to their establishment and acting under this impression were hardly conscious of what they were doing.

Indeed, it began to look as though they might so block the narrow passage with the stuff they sought to salvage that no one could either get up or down. Jack was finding it difficult to push past and had almost to climb over a bulky bundle of bedding that had become lodged in the passage.

Perk, more impetuous, bowled over a stout man who had come down the stairs dragging a trunk, that banged and skittered in a dangerous fashion.

By great good luck and the exercise of some muscle, they both managed to brush past the blockade and the stairs seemed free above them. The first landing was reached and the second almost immediately afterwards; then came the final climb and the two pals, almost breathless, reached the third floor.

There was enough illumination for them to see what lay about them for the fire seemed to be breaking out of all the upper windows by this time and despite the thick smoke, shone through into the interior of the brick tenement.

Smoke had found entrance too, and made their eyes smart but that was a small matter and could be tolerated with such a vital stake in view.

Perk saw his companion take a swift look around as though to get his bearings, after which he turned to the left and ran along the hall. By this time Perk, a bit bewildered and confused, was willing to follow wherever Jack saw fit to lead, so in blind confidence he put after the other.

A door stood open as if inviting the would-be rescuers to enter a room which Jack lost no time in doing, with Perk at his heels, both of them groping about amidst whirls of pungent smoke.

One of the two windows was open, which would account for the presence of that dense blanket and like a shot Jack jumped over to thrust out his head so as to ascertain whether his guess had been worth while.

He saw the greedy banks of flame shooting out, across and up, and felt it almost scorching his cheeks but just the same it was a satisfaction to discover he was exactly opposite the third window from the end of the burning building.

"This the right place?" Perk was booming in his ear for what with the roaring of the fire, the pumping of the steamers down below and the shouts of deeply interested crowds in every quarter, the clamor was indeed something fierce and impressive, stirring the blood in their veins and causing their hearts to beat wildly.

"Yes — that window right across this gap, Perk, is the one we picked out!"

"Je-ru-sa-lem crickets! I kinder guess I c'n make the riffle!"

Jack managed to catch hold of the reckless fellow as he was in the act of clambering up on the sill of the window, undoubtedly with the full intention of making a desperate attempt to jump across to the one from which the smoke was pouring forth.

"Don't think of trying it—a crazy idea—one chance in ten you'd get across without falling!" he shouted in the ear of the struggling one.

"Gosh! let me make the try, partner—sure I c'n do such a little stunt okay—let off, won't you, Jack?" pleaded Perk, but the other only tightned his grip.

"Even if you did manage to hang on and climb inside, what good would it do—how get the woman and child across the gap?" Jack roared, feeling that his comrade was losing all the sense he ever had.

Perk suddenly ceased struggling as though he had seen a great light.

"Wall, I guess you ditched me, ol' hoss — that's a fact they couldn't make it after all. Then what's to be done?" he went on to say, dejectedly.

"We've got to bridge it some way or other," snapped the ever ready Jack. "This is a kitchen, seems like, partner—jump into it now, and see if you can't run across something that would reach across to that other window—even an ironing-board might make it. I'll take a look across the hall, in some other apartment, and may run across another."

Perk, as if freshly inspired, set about his commission with alacrity and almost immediately made a plunge toward a corner of the small room to snatch up a six-foot board covered with several thicknesses of cloth that was scorched in numerous places as with a hot iron.

Jack had meanwhile darted into the hall, discovered another open door nearly opposite and without knocking rushed through to find a second deserted kitchen and not quite so much smoke to interfere with his vision.

Fortune again favored him, for almost the first object he saw was a similar ironing-board, evidently a mate to that Perk had run across.

Snatching it up he turned and hurried back to the opposite room, where he found Perk just laying his frail plank across the area to discover that it bridged the gap, although with but a mite to spare.

Jack arrived just in time for the rash one was in the very act of crawling out on his unsteady bridge which, if moved a few inches, would have precipitated him down thirty feet and more to land upon a cement pavement and meet with grievous injuries, even if he survived the drop.

"Hold on!" Jack shouted as he again caught hold of his chum. "Here's a second board that will widen the bridge. Let's swing it across and then one hold them together while the other crawls over!"

"Yeah, let's," Perk chimed in, seeing the advantage a double width would afford, and this was quickly accomplished.

"I'll go over," Jack was saying.

"Not much you won't — that's *my* job I'm tellin' you partner!" the other insisted, pushing Jack aside.

"But—I'm younger than you, Perk, spryer too—it ought to be my game, don't you see?"

"The devil you are!" whooped the one who would not be denied. "I'm stronger an' tougher'n you ever be, boy—an' I saw 'em first, too!

Let me have my way, *please,* partner, won't you?"

Jack, realizing that it would be the utmost folly for them to keep on disputing in this fashion while the very seconds were so valuable when human lives were in jeopardy, gave up the contention.

"All right, Perk, you win, but I'll go next time, remember. Make up your mind I'll keep the boards close together—be as easy as you can when crossing. Now, go to it!"

Already Perk was out on the strange bridge on hands and knees, crawling toward the opposite window while Jack, gripping the ends of the two boards with all his strength, held them steady. It was a tense moment and one not soon to be forgotten.

By this time it seemed that two of the firemen down below holding the nozzle of a hose and sending a stream of water up to the roof of the doomed tenement building had discovered what was being done, for they raised their hoarse voices to applaud the daring bridge creeper. It was all in the line of their own daily work and they surely could appreciate the venturesome act at its full value.

Jack had a dread lest they change the direction of the stream, hoping thus to sprinkle the climber and render him immune to that heat which they must know would be almost unbearable so close to those darting billows of fire but fortunately they did nothing of the sort, doubtless realizing how frail that mockery of a bridge must be and how the shock of a volume of water might cause it to break away.

A few seconds of dreadful suspense and then Perk vanished from view, having passed into the room through the third window from the end of the tenement. Jack almost ceased breathing, so thrilled was he lest that might be the last glimpse he would ever have of his pal.

CHAPTER IV

THE RESCUE

There was some sort of a movement across the way—then to Jack's great relief he saw Perk's head appear in the open window.

He had a small figure in his arms—the boy, undoubtedly and was already starting out upon the bridge. Jack could see no sign of life about the little child and had some fear that the rescue might have been too late to save him from being smothered by that dense smoke.

Just then he also discovered that another figure had appeared back of Perk, and readily guessed this must be the woman. She seemed to be holding the ends of the ironing boards as though possessed of a deadly fear lest they slip from the stone coping and precipitate both child and rescuer to their death in a wild plunge.

That caused Jack to tighten his own hold for Perk was having considerably more trouble in making his return than on his previous crossing since he now had to push the child ahead of him, being unable to navigate and hold a burden, however helpless, in his arms.

Again the firemen below were shouting words of praise and encouragement to the gallant soul that so fearlessly risked his own life for that of another. With them such exploits came in line with their duty, but in this case it was simply an act of humanity.

Jack waited until Perk had pushed the child against his hands, then cautiously he loosened his grip on the right board and dragged the light weight over the window sill to safety. Perk clambered in and immediately made a suggestive move as though about to turn around and do his stunt all over again but Jack refused to stand for such a thing.

"You've had your inning, buddy, so don't be hoggish," he bawled as he shoved Perk aside, "now it's my turn. Take hold, and keep the boards as steady as you can while I fetch the woman across."

Perk was very loath to obey and doubtless did a lot of grumbling, but Jack paid no further attention to him, just began to creep out on that narrow bridge, and move ahead inches at a time. He dared not look down lest it have some sinister effect upon his nerve—just kept his eyes firmly fixed upon that window toward which he was creeping.

The poor woman was still in sight, wringing her hands and yet evidently satisfied to know her child had been safely carried across the abyss that yawned there so threateningly. Jack would have liked to call out and beg her to keep quiet lest she chance to dislodge one of the frail supports upon which so much depended but he also feared lest he himself in thus shouting cause immediate trouble and defeat his purpose.

The crossing was made in safety. It was simply wonderful how those twin planks held together when the necessity was so great. Jack would never be able to look upon such an humble kitchen necessity again, whether in a house or a hardware store window display, without feeling warmly drawn toward the mute object on which his very life now depended.

He crawled through with a tongue of flame darting down and almost licking his cheek. It was necessary that he should get the woman to go out ahead of him, so that he could encourage her as they crept along.

"Steady yourself, madam," he called out as he felt her hands come in contact with his arm, "it's all right—your boy is safe, and you will be too if you get a grip on your nerve and do what I tell you."

She was evidently badly shaken as might be expected—he could see how she trembled and seemed so weak, which was why he spoke as he did, in the hope of putting a little new confidence in her almost fainting heart.

"You must crawl out ahead of me," he told her. "Don't look down—keep your eyes on the window where my pal waits for you—just keep saying to yourself that your boy is over there waiting for you—he needs you, and you must be brave now. There is no other way by which you can be saved to join him again. Can you make the venture, lady?"

He used that last word almost inadvertently, yet already had he decided that she was indeed a lady, though poorly dressed and evidently under financial difficulties.

He must have inspired his charge with some of his own valor, for he saw her cease trembling and knew full well it had been his mention of a reunion with her child that had effected this change.

"Yes, oh yes, I will be brave—for Adrian's sake, my baby boy!" he heard her cry as she started to creep out of the window amidst all that smoke and the devilish tongues of fire that darted after her as if in rage at being cheated of their intended prey.

Carefully did Jack follow after her, ready to throw out a helping hand should she make the slightest slip and be in danger of falling. But to his surprise and delight as well, she seemed to be supported by some miraculous power for she made the short passage without a single mishap.

Perk made no effort to drag her through the opening—to do so he would have had to take his hands from his job of holding the ends of the planks and this might lead to a sudden shift that would bring about the very disaster he had been dreading. His one thought now was the safety of his pal—the woman was capable of passing over the sill of the window without any assistance.

When, therefore, Jack came over the bridge-head and landed on the floor, the impulsive and thrilled Perk threw his arms about him, words failing him just then.

"We must get out of this," Jack managed to say, as soon as he could catch his breath again, "the fire is almost sure to jump across that gap and start things in this building unless firemen climb up here and hold it in check. Perk take up the child, who I see is beginning to come to all right. I'll help his mother down the stairs. We're all safe and sound, lady, so keep as nervy a front as you can."

Perk cuddled the little chap to his breast and Jack was tickled to see the boy clasp his own chubby arms around the other's neck as though he realized something of what Perk had done for him and loved him for that.

The descent was made slowly for there was more or less danger of one of them slipping and having a bad fall—but presently the last flight of narrow rear stairs had been negotiated and they came to the open door that led into the alleyway and safety.

They were just in time too, for a party of fire-fighters with a slack hose were just entering the brick tenement, evidently with the intention of dragging it to an upper window where, with the water turned on, they could fight the hungry flames at close quarters and at least keep the second building from being involved in the common destruction.

Perk might have been bothered to know what next to do but not the versatile Jack who led the woman out of the crowd and then looked around for some vehicle in which she and the boy could be taken to a hospital, for he had discovered that one of her arms seemed to hang at her side, as though it may have been broken in the excitement.

Fortunately a taxi chanced to come along into which they all bundled and were taken to the hospital. The boy sat in Perk's lap and his preserver seemed to take positive delight in holding one of the little chap's hands. Noticing how fond Perk seemed to be of children—and this was not the first time he had learned of this fact, since he had one of his humorous smiles for almost every child—and dog—he met—Jack wondered why his elder pal had never married but that was a subject Perk never mentioned nor had Jack felt it his province to make inquiries, since there are some things that are no one's business.

A doctor quickly examined the mother's arm and admitted that one of the bones was fractured. It was not a bad break, however, and she could be around with her arm in a sling after he had attended to it.

Somehow, although as yet supperless, neither of the chums seemed in any hurry to get away. Perk was held by his attraction toward the chubby little boy and as for himself he felt concerned with regard to what the pair they had saved would do, since they no longer had a home and all of their scanty possessions must have been devoured by those greedy flames.

He determined not to abandon them until he had learned how the mother was fixed with regard to this world's goods. Somehow, although she dressed very simply, there was an air of refinement about her that impressed Jack very much and he also had an idea she could not be in straightened circumstances for she was wearing a ring of considerable value, he noticed.

He managed to enter into conversation with

her after she had tried to tell him she would never forget what he and his friend had done for her that night. He had listened with his customary smile, shaking his head meanwhile, as if to belittle their actions.

"We could not have done less, after we saw that the firemen had not placed any ladder up to that third floor," he went on to tell her. "And then, you see my chum here, who lives only for excitement, was just complaining that things were so humdrum and dull so it tickled him to have a chance to test his nerve again. And you can see he's especially fond of little boys, not girls. We expect to leave Salt Lake City any hour now as we are aviators,—flying men you know—and have a job ahead of us. Before saying goodnight to you, madam, would you mind telling us if we can be of any further assistance to you and your fine boy here—pardon me for mentioning it, but are you supplied with present funds, since possibly you may have to remain here in the hospital for a week or more?"

She looked at him and smiled as though pleased with the solicitude he showed but she shook her head and hastened to say:

"We are not what you would call poor, for we have good friends back of us. Indeed, it was my intention to start for Spokane tomorrow as I must try to find a certain party whose present whereabouts means everything to me. So please do not worry about us, for we can get on. It was a furnished flat we occupied and while I have lost all my clothes as well as those of Adrian, that lack can easily be replaced. I thank you for your card giving me your Washington address. Some day perhaps you may hear from me and possibly I shall have some pleasant news to tell you but just now it is all wrapped up in mystery. So much depends on my finding the one who does not dream of the information we are carrying to him. If only my clue proves trustworthy."

That was as much as Jack learned and it was bound to often come up in his mind, causing him to wonder what the "good news" she mentioned could be.

CHAPTER V

AT THE FLYING FIELD

It was pretty late when they sat down to supper that night but as Jack had predicted, the appetite of his chum was amply recompense for the delay. They had done a good deed and best of all managed to get away before any inquisitive newspaper men arrived at the hospital on the track of a sensational beat.

"Which pleases me a whole lot," Jack went on to say as they started eating.

"Same here ol' hoss," added Perk, with unction. "Once them chaps get on the scent o' a good story they never do let up till it's spread out on the front page after bein' blue-penciled by the city editor. I know how it's put through, 'cause I got some pretty good friends in the bunch—they're all wool an' a yard wide on everything 'cept pokin' their noses into the private affairs o' citizens and couples that jest *can't* get on in double harness."

"Just imagine what a nasty shock it'd be to us both Perk, to see our names and pictures staring at us under a scare line of black type—yes, and like as not with as much as they could scrape together about our private business—nice way to upset all the plans of Secret Service hounds on the trail of big game, I must say."

"Honest, I didn't give away a single thing, buddy," said Perk with unusual earnestness, which was as good as an invitation for Jack to clear his skirts of the same suspicion, which he hastened to do.

"I simply gave her my address in Washington —at my room, you understand, Perk—I wanted her to write to me later on so we could know how they both came out after that nasty squeeze play. Not a whisper what line of business we followed and I asked her as a particular favor not to let a single soul know who the two parties were to whom she and her boy owed their narrow escape from being trapped in that burning house. She said the name would never pass her lips and that she would write, after something she was bound to accomplish had been put through. Of course I couldn't even give more than a guess what that is, only she seemed dreadfully in earnest and I reckon it might be a reconciliation with her husband, Adrian's father."

Perk nodded his head solemnly.

"Huh! mebbe so, Jack, mebbe so, lots o' that sort o' trouble goin' 'round these days, seems like.

Now I wonder if you thought to ask what her name might be?"

"Queer that I didn't think to do that, partner," Jack told him with a little laugh. "I reckon I must have been a little absent-minded but that's nothing to us for chances are we'll never meet the lady again. How about you and the boy?"

"He told me his name, Jack, when he gave me this little picture he happened to have in his pocket—you see on the back it's got written, I guess by his Mom herself: 'Adrian, at six'; but tarnation take the luck if I ain't jest plumb forgot the last name he told me—somethin' like Burnham or Barnard—begins with a B, I'm dead sure—Buster, Bramley—Buttons—well, for the love o' mike I can't strike oil but it'll come back, given a little time."

"And I can see plain enough if it keeps on skipping you it's bound to keep you busy guessing right along," Jack was saying, for only too well did he know this little weakness on the part of his comrade. Perk was bound to keep on pounding away at that puzzle day and night, giving himself no rest until he either solved the riddle or else some one told him the answer—left to himself he would never give up trying.

"Like as not, buddy," replied Perk, frowning darkly;" seems I'm gettin' up a tree every little while — never could remember names

worth a cent but I don't forget faces, you understand."

"And then too, you're a great hand for remembering to hear the first sound of the dinner
bell," said Jack with a chuckle.

"I sure am some punkins 'bout that," admitted
the amiable Perk with one of his goodnatured
grins spreading over his homely face.

"What's the program after we've cleaned up
this mess, eh partner?" inquired Jack, who
doubtless could make a good guess from previous
experience as to what his companion's answer
was apt to be, but for once he counted without
his host.

"Wall," observed Perk shaking his head, "I
did mean to take a look in at the pictur house,
seein' they got my ol' favorite, Milton Sills
booked tonight but shucks! it's too late an' 'sides,
somehow I kinder lost my likin' for action jest
now—mebbe I got my fill in that busy bee ses-
sion with the fire fiend down by the tenement
district—kinder a bit lame in the arm muscles,
so I figger on rubbin' 'em with my salve that
worked so fine after my rough landin' away back.
Yep, I'll cut out the movies for one night in
port an' go to bed early."

"I'm meaning to pick up all the extra sleep
possible," ventured Jack at which his mate
nodded approvingly.

"I get you," partner," he hastened to say, "kinder figgerin' on our skippin' out any ol' time an' like as not runnin' up against a rough passage that'll keep us on the jump. But I sure would like to have even an inklin' which way that hop-off's goin' to lead us."

"I'm surprised at such a reckless, devil-may-care sort of chap as I've known you to be, Perk, bothering your poor nut about such a silly thing just as if it mattered two cents to either of us which way we head—nothing ought to give us a second thought except that we're ready to jump in and carry through, any old place under the sun."

"Yeah! but then what'd I find to worry 'bout if I didn't pick on the way we're kept in the dark up to the last minute?"

Jack looked at him blankly and shook his head as if such peculiar philosophy were too much for him to master—then he changed the subject and the meal went on until even Perk, with his tremendous cargo capacity, could contain no more.

They sat in their room reading until their eyes getting heavy warned them it was time to hit the hay, as Perk was so fond of calling the act of getting into bed.

In the morning they were both astir, for it so

happened that neither had ever shown signs of being late sleepers, save on special occasions.

"Another day," remarked Jack while leisurely dressing, for since they had nothing afoot (save to possibly take a few hours' spin in order to keep in practice as well as test out several new devices with which they had as yet not become as familiar as Jack would like), there was no necessity for any hurry.

"An' wouldn't I give somthin' if only I knew we could check out before sundown tonight," grumbled Perk, yawning and stretching as though life was becoming entirely too tame and monotonous to satisfy his cravings.

"Wait and see," advised his chum, "you know the old saying that it's always darkest just before dawn—we're due to get a thrill before many more hours. Give Headquarters decent time to cook up a fine fat game for us, a nut to crack that'll be worth going after. I've a few little things on my list that I mean to carry out this morning when I'll be ready for the call."

Perk seemed unusually slow that morning, though he did not complain about his lame muscles. Even when Jack asked about it he shrugged and with a grimace remarked indifferently:

"Oh! that's okay, buddy—turned out to be a

false alarm—nothin' the matter with me, I guess, except I need shakin' up a wheen."

"You'll get all you want of that I reckon before you're many days older," Jack told him, "somehow I've got a notion we're going to be sent on a wild goose chase that may cover some thousands of miles and take us into a queer section of country—nothing but a surmise, or what you might call a *hunch* to back me up in that, remember, but I've known a hunch to come true more than a few times."

"I wonder," Perk observed dreamily, eyeing his comrade as if he again felt the old suspicion arise with regard to Jack knowing more than he chose to tell just then.

But unseen by either of the two pals, coming events were hurrying along and threatening to speedily engulf them in as dizzy a spin as either had ever encountered in all previous experiences.

It was around eight when they arrived at the flying field, as usual a scene of considerable bustle with ships coming in and departing—air mail carriers, visiting boats taking off in a continuance of their prearranged flights east or west and several heavier bombing planes that were being taken to Los Angeles by naval pilots for some secret purpose of the War Department.

Jack and his pal observed all this with grins

of sheer enjoyment, so bred in the bone had their love for their profession grown to be that everything connected with flying drew them as the Polar star does the magnetic needle of a compass.

"Times are getting right lively around these diggin's," remarked Perk, with a sparkle in his eyes and enthusiasm in his voice.

"Seems like it," replied Jack who chanced to be watching a novice just then starting out on what appeared to be his initial solo flight. "That boy shows fair promise of being due to break into the ranks of express pilots after he's had another hundred miles or so of flying. I like the way he handles himself and the test pilot told me yesterday he was sure to be a comer."

"Ol' Bob ought to know what's what," mentioned Perk taking a look for himself, "there, he's off and see how he lifts the ol' bus when he's ready. I watched him make as neat a three-point landin' yesterday as anybody could wish. A few o' 'em seem to be born with wings—but not many, not many, I'm sorry to say. Well, let's step over and get things started."

Perk stopped short as though some one had given him a blow—he seemed to be holding his breath while he stared and then commenced rubbing his eyes in a peculiar fashion, just as though he imagined he must be seeing things where they could not possibly exist.

Jack realized that his chum must have had a shock of some kind, and turned upon him quickly.

"What's the matter—what ails you, Perk?" he demanded.

"Gosh amighty! Jack, looky there will you—the hangar—Mister Gibbons; you know, where we parked out boat—it's burned down last night!"

CHAPTER VI

A BLOW IN THE DARK

Jack was naturally intensely shaken by this outburst from his companion. His first act was to whirl around and look hastily in the quarter indicated where he discovered quite a bunch of men clustered around some object from which wisps of smoke seemed to still be rising on the clear morning air.

He and Perk exchanged startled looks as though the same sudden thought had gripped their hearts.

"Queer I didn't notice a thing before, Perk, though I saw a crowd gathered—but then that's a common occurrence out here where so many interesting things keep on happening. Sure enough, the Gibbons' hangar has gone up—such accidents don't come along often in any modern aviation field."

"Accidents!" blurted out Perk steaming up— "lay off that stuff, ol' hoss—ev'ry little movement has a meanin' o' its own—up to last afternoon it was our ship that snuggled in that hangar, don't forget that, my boy. Talk to me 'bout luck, we hit it sky-high that time. Let's go see what's happened, and how they talk 'bout it in the bargain."

This proposal Jack was only too willing to stamp with his approval so they hurried toward the bunch of men — pilots, mechanics, visitors and riffraff chancing to be at the field just then and now engaged in staring at the ruins of the new hangar, doubtless exchanging opinions as to how the conflagration had occurred in the dead of night.

"Huh!" Jack heard his comrade saying as if to himself as they approached the cluster of men, "seems like we got up against a reg'lar roundup o' fire—last night that tenement, an' now today the hangar we been usin' to shelter our boat. Hot ziggetty dog! but ain't life queer though?"

Everybody was turning to stare at them as they came along. Undoubtedly it was generally known that their ship had been stored in the destroyed shelter while Mr. Spencer Gibbons was away and that it was only on the preceding afternoon on coming back from a flight that they had transferred it to another hangar Jack had been able to hire since the owner of the one they had been using had wired he would be home shortly after dark.

"When and how did this happen?" Jack asked one of the pilots as he took in the fact that the remains of a plane could be seen amidst the wreckage — apparently an explosion had taken place, for much of the charred material of which the hangar had consisted was scattered around the near vicinity.

"They tell us around about midnight," came the answer for the pilot knew Jack as a fellow craftsman, although a stranger to Salt Lake City aviation circles. "The alarm was given by the pilot of an incoming mail ship making port hours late on account of heavy fog in the mountains. Queer, too, they say, how quick it all came about—fire was blazing furious like when discovered, and nothing could be done to save Mr. Gibbons' fine ship. There he is yonder, talking to some newspaper boys."

Jack went over to tell the other how he was shocked to see what had happened to his property and to ask if anything was known as to the origin of the conflagration.

"Seems to be pretty much a mystery, they all tell me," the genial sportsman informed him, not showing any signs of being at all worried although undoubtedly deeply mystified. "You fellows were in some luck to get your ship out before this nasty thing came along which I'm glad to know. Of course I'm well insured and can replace my Pitcairn Mailwing readily enough, only I'd gotten that one working like magic. I'm glad no other hangar caught when mine burned. I've offered five hundred dollars for any information that will prove that this was a set-up job for it happens that on one other occasion something similar to this came my way. You see, I was unlucky enough to make a few enemies in Wall Street who've never forgiven me for knocking them out on a big deal."

Mr. Gibbons laughed and seemed in no wise bothered by his recent loss, only Jack noticed how his eyes seemed to glint like sparks from steel when mentioning the fact that he had unscrupulous enemies in the commercial world.

Jack hung around for some little time, talking to several of those present and asking numerous questions but learning next to nothing. If, as some of the ground attendants seemed to believe, it was an incendiary act, those who took big chances in carrying it out must have planned carefully and fixed matters not only to make a certainty of the ship sheltered within the hangar being destroyed, but also covering their tracks with great skill.

Finally he started over to the other hangar and Perk, seeing him go pulled his freight, as he would have called it, to hasten after his chum.

"Huh! looks like a fine sight for sore eyes," Perk declared with glee, "to see our boat standin' there safe an' sound tho' I'm sure sorry Mister

Fitzgibbons—I mean Gibbons, had to lose his crate—no fault o' ourn I'll tell the world, Jack."

"To be sure we could hardly be blamed for what happened," returned the other with a deep meaning in his voice and manner that caused Perk to start and then blurt out:

"By jinks! partner, does it look to you like some crazy snooper set fire to the hangar under the belief that our ship was locked in there?"

"Between you and me and the lamp-post, buddy, that just struck me as possible, though I've no proof to back me up in saying it."

"Another o' them slick hunches o' yourn, eh partner?" Perk hastened to say and then, scratching his chin in a way he had when seriously considering some debatable proposition that puzzled him very much, he added: "can't for the love o' mike guess how anybody could learn jest who an' what we might be but it's a risky line we're engaged in, buddy, an' some o' these here smart crooks have accomplices they say even in the service o' Uncle Sam. It's possible a whisper leaked out an' havin' some fish to fry, word was sent to some o' the big gang out here at Salt Lake City to do for us, or wipe our ship off the face o' the earth instanter. Gee whiz! but that sure does make things look mixed-up for us, ol' hoss."

"For one thing," said Jack, firmly, "after this

I never mean to leave our boat in a strange hangar without hiring a guard to watch over it every hour of every night, no matter what the cost to Uncle Sam. I reckon they keep some insurance on these crates, but it would be what time and instruments and charts we lost that would knock us the hardest."

"But how could anybody know what sorter job we're goin' to wrestle with next, even 'fore we got a glimmer o' it ourselves?" querulously demanded the bewildered Perk, up in the air again apparently for there seemed to be a vast number of things of which he was densely ignorant.

Jack laughed and shook his head.

"Some fine day perhaps we'll get on the inside track of these strange doings, brother but right now I'm just as much in the dark as you. All I know is that for some little time rumors have been going around at and close to Headquarters but so far as I understand the matter up to lately, the mysterious party responsible for such give-aways hasn't been located. So it's within the bounds of reason for me to suspect we've fallen under the ban and have had some sort of secret enemy set on our track."

"Huh!" snorted Perk indignantly, "kinder like that Oswald Kearns employed one o' his critters to do us a bad turn—you know, that big rum-runner we nailed down in Florida not so very long back an' whose trial hasn't come along so far, we've heard."

"Just like that," Jack told him, "although I hardly believe it could be any of his dirty work. Still, it's going to pay us to keep our eyes peeled right along and never imagine the coast is clear just because we don't happen to see any ugly character around. Such scamps usually manage to hide themselves daytimes, to slip out after dark and do their tricks.

Soon afterwards they had tooled their ship to the runway close at hand, made the dash, and started skyward like a bird. For two hours they tried out various capers so as to make certain they had complete control of the wonderful amphibian that had been placed at Jack's disposal by those at the Secret Service Bureau in Washington, intent on equipping their trusted agents with the best going, so that no failure might be laid at their door due to insufficient backing.

They were back again by one that same afternoon, it being against Jack's better judgment to remain away more than a few hours at a time. He knew that at any day a message from Washington, in secret cipher, was apt to come along and which, for aught he knew, would call for them to start out without any unnecessary delay and he wished to be on hand to receive it.

To save time he and Perk dropped into the dining room of the hotel without visiting the office so they might have dinner before going up to their room. This was pretty much of a daily habit with them and so far there had not been any disadvantage arising from the arrangement.

They had almost finished their dessert when one of the bellhops came along and being familiar with the pair from rubbing up against them so often, he asked no questions but laid down a telegraph envelope addressed to Mr. John Jacob Astorbilt.

"Gosh!"

That was all Perk could gasp when he saw that presumably the orders they had been expecting for so long must have arrived. He watched Jack reach out and pick up the sealed envelope—noted that there did not seem to be the slightest quiver of his hand — indeed, if it were an ordinary dunning epistle Jack could not have acted more carelessly — so far as outward manifestations showed—than was the case just then.

He opened the envelope and then, still as cool as a cucumber grown in the shade of a cornstalk, drew out the enclosure which Perk's devouring eyes told him was unusually long.

Food was quite forgotten—for once—by the enthralled Perk who sat there, fascinated, watching Jack's face as though in anticipation of being able to tell from what he might read there something of the nature of the communication that had been telegraphed from far distant Washington.

It was quite useless, however. Had Jack been glancing over a casual invitation to some party he could not have evinced more unconcern. Of course the message was so fashioned that in order to glean its full meaning a recourse to his code would be necessary but then as Perk knew, Jack would be able to pick up a word here and there and in this way get an inkling as to its purport.

CHAPTER VII

PERK HEARS THRILLING NEWS

"On your way, partner—gimme a clue to save me from crashin'!" begged poor Perk, his wits in a huddle that would have made any football enthusiast take a back seat.

"It's our order to get busy, okay," said Jack with a gleam in his eyes his pal loved to see, since it meant *action* and plenty of it.

"Where bound, for the love o' mike?" continued the other.

"I've made out one name here which may be our destination, Perk."

"Yeah?"

"Spokane," he was told at which Perk lifted his eyebrows as if to denote more or less surprise, likewise disappointment.

"Huh! 'bout a short day's flyin' from this joint," was the way the ambitious Perk voiced his feelings, just as if his expectations had been taking wings and soaring across the Pacific or some such long distance.

"Go slow, brother," his mate advised him, "give me half a chance to make this puzzle out

—so far I've caught just a word or two here and there. From the size of this message there's a heap back of it. If you're done stoking, let's pass up to our den where I can get out my code and decipher this thing."

Perk was out of his chair in a jiffy.

"I'm with you, laddie so let's get a move on. I kinder guess now I'll jump out o' this here lowdown fit in a hurry, once we get goin'."

He already looked a hundred per cent more awake than he had been for several days and Jack chuckled as he led the way to the elevator, knowing how new life had been pumped into his chum's veins by the receipt of the order to go.

Once seated in the room they shared in common, Jack took his secret code from its hiding place and set to work in earnest. Perk could see him writing down word after word and filling in vacant places. The minutes fairly dragged like lead to the impatient one and when Jack sat back, nodding his head as if wholly satisfied, the other again begged him to lift the lid and give him a peep-in.

"What's the matter at Spokane? Some o' them Bolshevik miners broke loose over in Idaho an' threatenin' to kick up general hell again like they've done so many times?"

"A rotten guess brother," Jack told him. "Nobody said we were going to stop long at Spokane

—just ordered to look up a certain party there who'd pass on a bunch of information he's been collecting this long while back and so help us on our way."

Perk beamed again, as though quite a load had been lifted from his chest.

"Sounds better to me, ol' hoss," he hastened to say. "An' tell me, where do we go from Spokane?"

"Due north!" snapped Jack smilingly, "in the direction of an old stamping-ground of yours."

"Across the border—into Canada, partner?" demanded Perk.

"Just where we'll be aiming for and more-over, buddy seems to me I've even heard you speak of a fur-trading post known as Frazer's, with a Scotchman as factor of the Hudson Bay Company, name of McGregor!"

At that Perk let out one of his whoops as though unable to contain his overpowering de-light.

"Ol' Jimmy McGregor you mean, Jack! Don't I know him from his moccasins up, the queerest but straightest man in the whole North-west Territory? Why, I was located not many miles away from his store an' many a time dropped in to get my 'baccy at his counter. I'll be as happy as a lark to shake his honest hand again. Now wouldn't that jar you though—such great luck?"

"Here's another name you may chance to know. We're to pick up one of the Mounties at the post and take him along as a sort of guide and backer, so as to show we're playing our game in conjunction with the legal authorities of the region. Ever meet up with Sergeant Lowden, Perk?"

"Say, I was in cahoots with a mighty fine lad by that name," came the speedy reply, "but if it's *him* they've given Red a big boost since I quit the game and went back to flyin'."

"That sounds good to me, just the same," Jack told him, "because we're set to see a heap of the Sergeant before we skip back to our own side of the border and with him being an old pard of yours it's likely he'll feel it's up to him to do his level best to help us corral that wildcat."

"Meanin' who, if it's all the same to you, partner?" Perk observed.

"Listen then and get it pat, brother. Some time last year a certain man escaped from Leavenworth Penitentiary — it's never been learned just how he managed it, or who on the outside or in gave him a lift. Seems that he was a man Uncle Sam particularly wanted to keep shut up for a long term—a dangerous man to be at large. This brought about a bunch of trouble at Washington, and a number of high officials felt the finger of suspicion. Lax methods and such, you understand, being leveled at them. Rewards have been posted everywhere and I can remember seeing several of them in my travels, but up to now never has the first bit of information filtered in to Headquarters. They seemed to infer from certain hints that the escaped prisoner had gone West, but then again it was said he had skipped to South America where he could change his name and keep on playing hob with other people's wealth. His name, Perk, before he was hauled in and sent to the pen was Leonard Culpepper!"

"Hot ziggetty dog! so, *that's* the way the scent leads us, is it?" cried Perk, evidently fully aroused by the disclosure. "Sure, I've seen them posters in mor'n a few post offices north an' south, east an' west and wondered who'd be the lucky dick to snatch that fat reward they put up. Gee! you've got me near goofy partner, with that news."

"Listen again then, Perk, and get the gist of what this message has given to us. Information had trickled in through several sources to state positively that a man answering the description of Leonard Culpepper has been playing hob up in the Northwest Territory for some months now. He's got a few tough bad men he runs with and they take their orders from him. That's another proof of his identity, since Leonard never would play second fiddle to any living man. It was rule or ruin with him every time."

"Huh! gettin' hotter right along I'd say, Jack —suits me to a dot, an' sure worth waitin' for in the bargain," and if any one could judge how happy Perk felt just then, the grin on his face, as well as the way in which he kept rubbing one hand over the other, just like a miser gloating over his gold, would be enough to tell the tale.

"Remember, boy, this man is reckoned a desperate character, ready to go to any extreme to keep his liberty. Even your old comrades the Mounties have so far fallen down on the job of taking him in. He seems to play too slick a game for the whole posse and we understand that at least one officer has mysteriously disappeared when trying to track him to his lair. So make up your mind we'll have to match wits with even Sherlock Holmes if we hope to get the better of this hard hitter."

"What's the name he goes by up there?" asked Perk.

"No name at all — they call him the *Hawk,* because he swoops down on his prey unawares and is absolutely merciless. Two gold prospectors who were said to have struck it rich somewhere further north have disappeared and it's suspected they fell in a fight with his gang. Sometimes he's here and in a few days they tell of him bobbing up a hundred miles away."

"Jest like a flea," suggested Perk, "gone afore you c'n put a finger on him. Wall, I kinder like the way our job's laid out for us, partner. The bigger they are the harder they fall when Uncle Sam's men get goin'. So we're meanin' to pick up a bunch o' news at Spokane, are we? An' if it's a fair question, ol' hoss, *when* do we cal'late to pull out o' this burg?"

"No particular hurry, understand, Perk, we can take our own time going—slow and sure is to be our motto. But I'm a little like you in wanting to make a start, then, if we feel so disposed, we can loaf a while or turn aside if we see a chance to play a trick for Uncle Sam. That gives us a lot of leeway, you see."

"Nearly two o'clock right now—c'n we get off this afternoon, partner?" hinted the anxious one, appealingly.

"By four we ought to be on our way, buddy. Now let's get busy!"

CHAPTER VIII

THE TAKE-OFF

Jack was sorry that, owing to their pulling out so soon, he would not be able to visit the hospital again as he had planned and upon mentioning this fact to his companion, Perk shrugged his shoulders as he said:

"That's a down right shame, I'd say, partner, fact is, I depended on you to find out what Adrian's last name was—save me a wheen o' worriment if on'y I knowed it—somethin' that rhymed with Barnum — Bernard — Burling — Berwind—hang the luck, jest *why* does this ol' short memory for names bob up to bother a feller when we're startin' off on a big spin an' may never see thet lady an' little Adrian again? Seems I'm jest goin' to speak the right word, an' then, shucks! it misses connection like, an' leaves me a gropin' in the dark."

Jack, being accustomed to his pal's queer ways, did not take much notice of the new cause for worry that had gripped the stubborn one. He felt pretty certain he would see Perk sitting many times with a brooding expression on his face and counting his fingers while checking off each and every name he could conjure up that sounded like Barnum, etc., to finally heave a tremendous sigh, shake his head and apparently try to get the troublesome puzzle out of his mind.

It was all very sad but then one usually has to pay some sort of penalty because of having a poor memory for names.

As for Jack, he gave the subject little thought partly because he had matters of much greater moment to take up his attention. Indeed, he would have been considerably surprised could he have suspected how that name for which Perk was grappling just through his stubborness, would play quite an important part in those adventures which they were destined to run up against on the other side of the Canadian border.

"Now let's forget everything that happened last night," he told his chum seriously, "and stick to our business which is connected with the bringing in of that fierce go-getter and all-round bad egg who slipped out of jail so mysteriously that the wardens are floundering in a bog up to this day. All of which proves he's no easy mark and that we'll have to be on our toes if we expect to cage our bird."

They were so well prepared for the sudden emergency call that little remained to be done. The crate was serviced and could cover fully fifteen hundred miles as the crow flies with the gas they had aboard. Then, too, as they figured on stopping over in Spokane possibly a day or so, there would be ample opportunity to refill their aluminum tanks to the limit as well as lay in such other necessities as occurred to them.

"We've got to remember," remarked cautious Jack as they were heading for the flying field before two that afternoon, "that once we start across the line, we'll have few chances to fill up with gas. They may happen to have some gas at the post, or perhaps the Mounties could supply us because in these days of much flying it would be possible for a ship to drop down near by and be in need of fuel so badly the pilot would pay a big price to be supplied but I don't mean to bank on such a happening."

"Huh! mebbe things have changed some since I served with the Mounties," Perk went on to say; "for there wasn't such a thing as a gallon o' gas within fifty or a hundred miles o' the post at that time. Folks are gettin' air-minded ev'rywhere you go today an' it wouldn't surprise me to find they've got some sort o' a landin' place close at hand. Ain't staggered at anything nowadays, buddy."

They lost no time in reaching the field and as it was a pleasant day they found it an animated scene, with crates coming and going, visitors as well as those connected with the field in some capacity helping to make up a crowd with scores of spectators as a backing, rushing from one point to another.

This thing was such an old story for both flyers they paid little attention to the bustle that was going on but made straight for the hangar where their ship was quartered.

Jack had kept his word and a man could be seen standing or moving about near the squatty building. This was a guard in his employ, engaged by the day, for an indefinite time. It might be a week or a day, depending on the whim of the young and ardent sportsman, whom it was believed meant to hunt big game somewhere within five hundred miles of Salt Lake City.

"Listen Perk," said Jack as they approached the hangar, "it might be just as well for neither of us to say a word about making a quick run of it until about to pull out when I'll pay our man double wages. After what happened here last night anything might come along to upset our calculations."

"I'm on Jack—seems like you never do know what's what these days. Any more light on who did that dirty, sneaky job last night, eh what?"

"Nothing positive but I'm still of the opinion it must've been meant for us," replied Jack.

"Everything points that way for we happened to change our hangar with hardly anybody knowing about it. Then again I understood Mr. Gibbons dropped in along about nine and never a soul to meet him and his pilot save the customary field hands. But then there's no use crying over spilled milk—what's done can't be changed and it serves to warn us never to trust to just mixing up our names. We've got to believe there are just as smart wideawake chaps up against us as we ever claim to be. That'll be enough on the subject Perk, so let's forget it."

"Anyway, luck's all in our favor, seems like," was the consolation Perk offered himself, at the same time relapsing into silence.

As quietly as possible, just as if they meant to take an ordinary spin, they got their bus out of the hangar. Jack had paid the rental for it in advance, so there was nothing to worry them from that quarter, which was just as well for things somehow manage to fly around among the employees and pilots connected with a base port and the news would soon become common property that the young millionaire sportsman and his pilot were at last on their way to some chosen hunting ground in search of big game like moose, grizzly bears or possiby Rocky Mountain bighorn sheep.

As usual Jack gave the ship the once over, to

make doubly certain nothing had been neglected. So far as he was able to tell it was in apple-pie condition and so well stocked that they could count on a two thousand mile flight unless baffled by storm or dense fog banks.

The guard was given double pay and told that his services would not be needed any further, since a sudden wire had changed their plans somewhat and they were pulling out for good. If he evinced any particular curiosity concerning the goal they had in view, never a word spoken by either of the flyers put him any the wiser. Not that Jack suspected he might be in touch with some mysterious but vindictive enemy, but just kept mum on general principles.

"All ready, partner!" sang out Perk in his usual happy fashion for it always pleased him beyond measure to be making a start on some new air voyage and from what Jack had told him, Spokane was going to be only a way station, with the vast unknown Northwest Territory beckoning them on to fresh activities and mayhap thrilling adventures to follow. No wonder the chap whose nerves were always set for action felt joyful when the moment came to pull the gun and swing off.

One last look around and aloft so as to stamp his approval on the conditions with which they were to be confronted, and Jack made the momentous start. The wonderful up-to-date amphibian began to move down the slight decline with constantly augmented speed until, having reached the desired maximum the pilot lifted his craft and away they soared.

Perk took a last backward look at the field that had become fairly familiar to them by this time. There was a grin upon his freckled face that told of the pleasure he felt at such an auspicious moment. A ship was just coming into port, settling down for the last glide—just as a duck might set its wings, and throw its webbed feet forward on nearing the surface of a lagoon on which it intended to alight.

Perk rather imagined it was a belated air-mail boat, delayed by some accident like a forced landing or unusual weather conditions. No matter, he waved a hand gaily in salute to the homecoming air-man and felt no ill humor because there was no return wave, since the one whose hand was at the stick must needs give his full attention to his work, or risk a crash.

So they departed from the friendly Salt Lake City airport, with a far distant goal in view.

CHAPTER IX

A BROKEN PADDLE

After attaining some thousands of feet altitude, Jack headed into the north-west-by-north, it being his intention for variety to follow the shore line of the water until near its extreme northerly tip. This was only done for a change and to please Perk, who had mentioned the fact that he would welcome such a brief run, being a bit tired of looking down on endless stretches of rough country, mountainous in most places and with a most monotonous panorama passing far below.

So after all it was accident rather than an expectancy of meeting up with any sort of adventure that brought about the rather odd happening falling to their lot that afternoon.

Perk having little to do just then that could not be deferred until later on, was amusing himself with the glasses, looking back toward the old Mormon city with its vast temple devoted to the service of the followers of Brigham Young and the many other interesting features which he and Jack had faithfully surveyed while they were killing time and awaiting orders.

When these sights began to grow dim in the distance, he swept the surface of the big sheet of salty water and noted far away toward the west the shoreline bounding it in that quarter.

The day that had begun with considerable warmth had also brought up clouds that had, Perk thought, a bit of menace in their dark depths. Perhaps after all they would be treated to a little thunder and lightning for a change but that did not give him any concern, since both he and Jack were used to meeting up with boisterous weather when in flight and knew all the practical wrinkles for avoiding discomfort under such conditions.

Through the glass he could easily make out the various towns and smaller places that were to be met with along the eastern shore of the winding lake. They interested him from time to time, especially since Jack for some reason of his own had seen fit to drop down until they were zooming along not more than two thousand feet above the lake itself.

"Some wind down there," remarked Perk suddenly. "Startin' to kick up the waves like it might mean business."

"I wouldn't be surprised if we got a fair-sized blow later on," Jack told him as their ear-phones had been adjusted in order to permit an exchange of opinions and also allow them to work in common.

Perk shot a look skyward and noticed the clouds were actually growing blacker and more menacing. But that meant nothing in his care-free life. If the wind began to bother them it would be a simple thing to climb above the storm and keep merrily on their way, leaving the overcharged clouds to deluge the land beneath with their contents.

Perk was very still for some little time and seemed to be paying particular attention to something that had attracted his notice.

"I say, partner," he suddenly said, and Jack could tell he was agitated for some reason or other.

"Yes, what is it, Perk?" demanded the pilot.

"I don't just like the looks o' it, that's what!" exclaimed the other.

"Nothing more than a summer squall, with some fireworks thrown in for good measure, Perk. I'm surprised at you, old man."

"You're gettin' me wrong, ol' hoss," burst out the other; "I ain't referrin' to the weather, which don't disturb me a whiff—it's that silly little canoe down yonder an' sure as shootin' it's a *gal* in it wavin' a white flag o' some kind!"

"What's that, boy?" cried Jack, startled somewhat by Perk's last words.

"A punkin-seed boat, such as no sensible person'd use on such a big sheet o' water as this here Salt Lake and she don't seem to have any paddle at work either, that I c'n see—mebbe now it's got broken an' thar she is three miles out from shore with the wind blowin' her further all the while!"

Jack had banked by this time and was commencing to circle preparatory to dropping down in a glide. Somehow what his mate had just said stirred his blood and without the first thought concerning their present errand he was listening to the call of humanity.

After all there was no need of undue haste while on this business of the Government. They had made the start, Perk's impatient mood had been successfully muzzled, and if they found occasion for any reason to delay their progress while en route to their distant destination, it would be all right.

"How about it now?" he sang out a little later when they had reached a ceiling of less than a thousand feet.

"Jest like I was sayin' partner," replied Perk promptly.

"It's a girl then?" asked the pilot.

"Sure is, an' a slip o' a youngster in the bargain, not over ten or twelve years old, I'd say on a guess. An' let me tell you, Jack, she's keepin' up that wavin' her flag like fun—guess now she's skeered we'll give her the go-by.

"We've got to drop down on the lake then, that's clear," said Jack, just as though it was imperative to attempt the rescue of the youthful castaway, once her serious plight had come to their notice.

"Some rough sleddin' for us, partner," mentioned Perk to quickly add: "But shucks! what o' that, with you holdin' the stick. Our boat c'n stand the racket okay. On your way, partner!"

Jack was now able to see for himself without the aid of glasses. There could be no question as to Perk having struck the absolute truth when he declared it was a question of life and death for the frightened occupant of the dainty little canvas canoe that was bobbing up and down in the rising waves like a floating cork. Yes, he could even make out what looked like a broken spruce paddle lying in the bottom of the tiny craft as though it had played the paddler a treacherous trick just when she needed it the most and been cast aside as useless.

He dropped still lower, with a practiced eye keeping tabs of the wind and waves that were being kicked up. Then came the contact between the pontoons and the roughening surface of the lake — a considerable commotion followed, but the admirably built aluminum floats did their expected duty and in a brief space of time they were safely established on the heaving waters, not more than thirty feet away from the young and distressed mariner.

Again the rat-tat-tat of the engine was heard as Jack turned on full power, knowing he had a combination of wind and waves to beat. The spray flew quite briskly and Perk let out one of his joyous whoops as, amidst all this clamor, they continued to taxi in the direction of the bobbing punkin-seed as he had called the drifting canoe.

The young girl had ceased waving the white object which Jack strongly suspected might be a piece of her own clothing, torn off in desperation when she feared her lone chance of rescue might pass by, leaving her to a cruel fate. She was kneeling in the tossing boat, staring toward the approaching strange craft—an airship that could navigate the lake as though by magic, something she undoubtedly had never witnessed before, even though planes must be a familiar sight, seen far up in the heavens as they journeyed back and forth on their individual errands.

So they soon came alongside the helpless canoe and Jack was telling his pal just how it would be best to get the girl aboard. Her craft of course would have to be abandoned, since it was out of the question for them to taxi head-on over that water, growing constantly rougher as the wind rose higher with the shore something like three miles distant.

After all the safety of the girl was the main thing they must keep in view — a canoe only represented a small amount of money but a human life was priceless.

Perk made ready to assist the wretched skipper of the frail craft aboard, although it required considerable maneuvering on the part of the pilot to fetch the ship around so that the contact could be effected. At the proper moment Perk reached out his hand and once he clutched that of the girl he knew the rescue was as good as accomplished, for he would never let go.

In this queer fashion then was a third inmate of the ship's cabin installed and the canoe allowed to drift away. The girl was too much agitated just then to bemoan the loss of her treacherous little shallop, for sinking down on her knees she burst into violent sobs the result of her late terror. But their main object had been attained and now to get out of this rough sea.

CHAPTER X

It turned out to be rather a wet job, forcing the amphibian along against the waves and the wind, constantly increasing in vigor and both of them, as well as the girl, were more or less soaked before sufficient speed could be attained to permit the boat to swing upward and take to the air. Superior skill accomplished Jack's end at last and they left the agitated surface of the lake to ascend and head toward the shore.

Of course there was no way of asking the questions Perk had on the tip of his tongue, since she could not possibly hear anything he might say, what with the clamor of motor exhaust and spinning propeller, together with the shrill whistle of the wind amidst the struts.

But then according to Perk's mind there was no need of hearing any explanation, for it was all so simple — the girl had foolishly ventured out farther than discretion warranted in such a frail craft then the sudden rising of wind and waves had alarmed her, and she must have plied her paddle with such good will that suddenly it had snapped in the middle where possibly a knot in the wood had proved to be its weakness, leaving her helpless far from land and with a storm gathering.

No wonder the poor child was frightened — any man might have felt a chill passing over him as he contemplated his slender chances of being saved. And strangest of all, it had been no rescuing boat from the shore that arrived in time to take her aboard, but an airship dropping down from the clouds in the most miraculous way that could ever be imagined.

It was now their bounden duty to get her ashore as quickly as possible, for probably her folks would have discovered that she was missing and filled with fears, were at their wits end to figure how they could discover her whereabouts and go to her assistance.

Imagine their amazement when looking far out over the heaving waters they discovered a sky-scraper zooming along, suddenly make downward swoops and presently float upon the lake, for what object they could only surmise and feed their sinking hearts with wild hopes. Then to see the airship again taking wing, and even head toward the land, must have filled them with a wild enthusiasm. Jack knew very well what sort of reception he and his chum would be apt to receive and was determined to avoid it if possible, even to the point of seeming un-mannerly. He could not enjoy the thought of being made to pose in the role of a hero when all they had done was of a most ordinary character.

"See that crowd gathering on that little dock —she pointed to it, an' tried to let me know it was where she came from."

Perk was calling in the pilot's ear as he himself thrust out his hand and called Jack's attention to the excited little group of gesticulating, waving people. The girl was once more making use of her distress flag, but now her face was lighted up with enthusiasm rather than flooded with despair for she must begin to feel like some fairybook maiden being brought safely back to her father's palace after being torn from the castle of the odious ogre—that is about what her sensations must be, Jack was telling himself, if she had a spark of romance in her makeup, which was very likely the case.

Jack went about carrying out his plans by cutting off the engine and gliding down toward the water, comparatively smooth so close to the shore for the wind just then was coming off the land.

They struck with a great splash and the impetus almost sufficed to carry the amphibian to the outer edge of the miniature wharf, suitable only for small boats. Eager hands were held out to the girl, already leaning far over and in danger of falling overboard in her desire to reach her dear ones. But zealous Perk kept hold of her until she could be drawn up by many willing hands to be fairly smothered with a multitude of kisses, the women in particular showing their enthusiasm in this regard.

"Push off!" Jack told his chum who was kneeling there, gazing at the riotous scene, his face decorated by one of his customary grins.

So it happened that a minute or so afterwards, when the tattoo of the working motor startled the group around the girl, to their astonishment and dismay as well, they discovered the rescuing airship moving rapidly away. In vain did they hold out their hands and beckon as though actually pleading to the airmen to come ashore and accept their warm thanks for saving the life of the one so dear to their hearts. Both Jack and Perk smiled, but only shook their heads in the negative as they passed further away from the little landing with its excited group.

There was Perk sending kisses back with all his soul and Jack could see that this was for the benefit of the little girl, who, pushing to the front of the milling crowd was blowing kisses after them, as if in her heart she must let them know how grateful she felt for what they had done.

That was quite enough for Jack—the memory

of the little deed would often arise in his mind and make him all the more satisfied that he had not waited to listen to the applause of those good people who must likely enough always believe it was about the only case on record where two gallant chaps who had actually done a creditable deed, refused to be lionized because of their modesty.

Perk was again paying some attention to the weather, for those black clouds seemed to be gathering thicker than ever toward the southwest and from the signs, it would not be difficult to prophesy the coming of a fairly savage summer storm.

"Going to be some buster, seems like to me, Boss," mentioned Perk with a hint in his voice as if he would be pleased to hear what his comrade thought of the proposition and likewise what course they should pursue in order to escape as much of the coming turmoil as lay in their power.

"Between you and me and the lamp-post, brother," Jack remarked a bit seriously, "I don't seem to hanker much about climbing in hopes of getting through all that black mess, it's got a venomous look to me as though it might turn out to be one of those electrical twisters we've heard about. I've half a mind to run in closer to the shore in hopes of finding some sort of a point heading out into the lake behind which we could run and be sheltered from the worst of the blow. How about that, Perk?"

"Sounds good to me, ol' hoss an' by the same token I kinder guess I just sighted the cape we want, a mile or so ahead there."

He pointed as he spoke to what looked like a fairly sizable point that jutted out from the shore and behind which they would undoubtedly find a lagoon deep enough for their purpose.

"Yes, I see what you mean and here we go licketty-split for that headland," Jack told him without loss of time.

Indeed, the grumble of distant thunder had by now grown more like a roaring lion or a bull alligator in a swamp, challenging a rival to deadly combat.

"The closer we get the better I like that cape," Perk was saying as he continued to stare through the glass, "it's pretty high land and ought to shield us fairly well from any blow I'm glad to say, 'cause the wings o' the best ship ever built are kinder weak stuff and likely to be blowed away in a gale when held fast by an anchor or hawser."

Jack was picking the proper spot on which to alight—of course that would be on the water, but then it would be an easy matter for them to taxi around the point and find a safe harbor if things were as they pictured them.

This program was duly carried out without the slightest difficulty. The friendly tongue of high land proved all they could have hoped for and Jack readily drove his boat around its tip, to bring up further on where the ground rose to its maximum height.

"Looks okay to me, Perk," he called out as he stopped his motor.

"Couldn't well be bettered I'd say, partner."

"Then drop the mudhook, and see what kind of holding bottom you get," Jack told his mate which Perk proceeded to do without loss of time.

Thus they found themselves apparently sheltered in safety behind a barrier that should hold back the riotous winds as well as the waves that would soon be beating heavily against it. With the cabin for shelter they would not have anything to complain about, unless the storm should turn into a regular cyclone and Jack could hardly conceive such a thing possible away out there on the shore of Great Salt Lake, far removed from the hurricane districts of the Mexican Gulf.

CHAPTER XI

A STORMY NIGHT

By this time the forerunners of the gale had arrived with considerable electrical display and reverberating thunder. Of course the two flyers had removed their ear-phones since the motor lay silent and the whirlwind propeller had also ceased to spin around with incalculable speed but when the thunder began to roar at its loudest they found it necessary to shout in order to make themselves heard.

"Say, promises to be some screecher, b'lieve me!" was the way Perk put it when an extraordinarily loud crash almost burst their eardrums, the preceding flash having seared their eyes and nearly blinded them.

"Some fireworks for a fact," conservative Jack admitted frankly, "didn't reckon on such an exhibition so soon. But see here, Perk——"

"Yeah!" snapped the other, showing his readiness to act if anything was needed along the order of further security from the rain that was now drenching the shore line as if a cloud had burst.

"Seems to me you're forgetting something, partner," continued Jack.

"As what, Boss?"

"Isn't it about time for *grub?*" demanded Jack whose face was set in a grin a sudden flash of lightning disclosed.

"Je-hos-i-phat! if that ain't the very first time I ever did forget such a thing as eats!" burst out the chagrined co-pilot. "That's a fact, it is our time for attendin' to the gnawin' down below-stairs. Wait up, buddy, an' I'll fix things up okay in a jiffy."

He was as good as his word, although the measure of action he mentioned has never as yet been exactly settled. Perk knew just where he had put his supplies and trotted them out with alacrity, likewise undoubted pleasure for that sacred rite of eating was one of the duties the war veteran always stood by manfully.

Undoubtedly both of them had partaken of meals under many peculiar conditions but if their comments had any bearing on the subject never before had they dined under such fright-fully noisy accompaniments as right then with the cannonading from heaven's heavy artillery constantly booming, the wind howling like a pack of maddened wolves and the waves smash-ing against that little rocky ridge that sheltered them so bravely.

Perk had lighted the stub end of a candle so that they might not be in complete darkness, for it was as though midnight had arrived, especially between the vivid flashes as streaks of lightning went zigzagging athwart the black dome overhead.

Calmly they continued to munch their sandwiches and take occasional sips of hot coffee from the thermos bottle, Perk having supplied a couple of large aluminum cups for the occasion.

"Don't seem to let up any that I c'n notice," remarked Perk later on when they had taken the edge off their appetites.

"Weather fooled me that time for certain," added Jack frankly, "but then I never did claim to be a good hand at guessing what was coming along in this line. Government reports have always served me decently and even they can't always be depended on. This upset may last most of the night for all we can tell."

"Who cares?" sang out Perk, gaily enough. "I worked in a boiler factory in my salad days an' got used to all kinds o' rackets. Nary a drop o' rain gets in here, you notice comrade, thanks to the swell cabin we've got over our heads. Huh! how many times have I gone through big storms in the open cockpit o' an old-fashioned crate. Been bombarded too aplenty by half a hundred big guns, with shells bursting every-which-way around.   Seems like a feller c'n git used to near anything if on'y he runs up against it often enough."

"Snug as two bugs in a rug," agreed Jack lightly.   "Here we'll stick it out tonight and go on after morning breaks—no hurry, remember, brother—just take things as they come along and keep in trim for the big push later on."

"That's the ticket, Jack, boy—it sure wins out in the end—no blunders, jest every move carried out like machine work an' we're sure to come in smilin' at the windup."

Later on there was a little letup in the violence of the storm and Perk even felt encouraged enough to predict that the worst was over with possibly a nice, peaceful night's rest ahead.

This, however, proved to be a false deduction on his part for once again the thunder rose to a deafening pitch, with a wind of such velocity that Jack himself felt a little uneasiness, not on account of his own security, but because of the great damage he fancied the surrounding country would suffer in consequence of wind and flood.

"Danged if the ol' thing ain't turned turtle on us an' got started on the back track agin!" complained the humbled Perk. "What I know 'bout weather you could stick in a thimble!"

"But you're wrong when you say it's backed

upon us," Jack told him pointedly, "for the wind is still coming from the same old quarter, this is only another section of the same old storm."

"Huh! running this train in sections are they?" continued the disgusted Perk, "wall, I on'y hope they ain't too many more parts to the contraption—I've seen quite enough a'ready."

Having finished their supper they made themselves as comfortable as the conditions allowed. Jack got to figuring, as usual, for he was a great hand at laying out his plans in black and white for reference when the time for action arrived. Perk was poring over some clippings he had picked up at some time or other and which appeared to be of special interest to him.

It was indeed a most eccentric storm, now waning and giving promise of expiring, anon picking up again and squeezing out considerable more water to help finish the flooding of the earth.

Tiring of his reading with a poor light, Perk had for some little time been lying there so quietly that Jack half suspected he might have passed into dreamland. Suddenly he gave a loud grunt and exclaimed:

"Reckon now it might be jest plain Barrowman—an' yet somehow that don't seem to sound quite right — how 'bout Baxter—Banister—Brockman—shucks! what ails me anyhow—my bean ain't worth a red cent when it comes to 'memberin' names—guess I must be goin' a bit loco an' next thing I know I'll have to sew my own name on my coat in case I forget it."

Jack only chuckled, knowing that his chum was going through the same old game of cudgeling his treacherous memory with the usual poor results as of yore.

Later still, and both of them seemed to get more or less sleep though the storm kept up a growling and threatening for hours, as if not content with such damage as it must have already done.

Finally Perk, aroused by signs of daylight, looked out and was highly pleased to discover that not only had dawn really arrived, but that there was not a single cloud to be seen in the entire heavens.

"Hi! partner, wake up!" he called out, "mornin's got here an' that pesky row-maker's cleared out for keeps—goin' to have a clear day for our flight to Spokane. After such a devil o' a blow I kinder guess we might look for fair stuff a hull week o' Sundays. But hold on, I forgot I was sech a poor weather sharp, so don't count on anything I might say—I jest don't know what they got laid up for us flyers, an' that's a fact."

They had a very decent breakfast, for Perk hunted up some dry wood, he calling himself a

Maine woods guide these days it appeared, and consequently able to skirmish suitable fuel, even after such a drenching downpour. Then, after starting a cooking fire he produced a light-weight skillet, also a pound of sliced breakfast bacon, some strips of which he proceeded to fry as though quite accustomed to playing the role of camp cook. Then too, he had a new aluminum coffeepot which he meant to christen on that occasion so the appetizing odors of these two breakfast mainstays soon spread around the entire community, doubtless much to the wonder of various chipmunks and red squirrels that frisked here and there among the trees.

Jack said nothing, only nodded his head at witnessing these wonderful revelations as if things suited him all right. Trust sagacious Perk to make ample preparations for the numerous meals they would have to count on while engaged in the future tasks certain to be given into their charge from time to time.

CHAPTER XII

THE LAY-OVER AT SPOKANE

There was no trouble whatever about getting off after Jack had checked his motor and the rest of their ship so as to make certain nothing had suffered during the sway of that extraordinary storm.

As they went along, still keeping above the lake shore much of the way, Perk frequently called out as he discovered by use of the binoculars some particular damage done by the unwelcome visitor of the preceding afternoon and night. Trees were down and obstructing the highway between the various towns—several houses he noticed appeared to have chimneys toppled over or, as was the case in one sad instance, have a tree fall directly on the roof and occasion considerable damage.

Presently they had left the lake in their wake and were also changing the line of their flight more or less. Jack had laid out his plan and felt positive of being able to strike their distant goal in due time, even if he did not have the beacons of the air-mail flyers to guide him.

Somewhere about noon they glimpsed a city ahead which of course must be none other than Spokane. Shortly afterwards they were circling above the aviation field and gradually lowering so as to strike the proper spot. In these air-minded times the coming of a strange plane no longer excited an undue amount of curiosity, since a multitude of private aircraft were daily scouring all sections of the country from Florida to the Canadian border and between both oceans —as Perk was fond of saying they'd soon become as common as dirt.

No sooner had they made contact with the ground than Jack, followed by his companion, jumped out to be greeted by several parties in the same class as themselves—pilots, mechanics and field workers. It was no trouble to get the use of a hangar, since there chanced to be several vacant ones for hire. So too did Jack see fit to engage a promising looking man to stand by their ship and make certain no one tampered with it. A good judge of faces, Jack felt certain he had picked out a dependable man for this duty so that his mind might be free from any worry while in the city attending to his particular business.

Perk, for some reason or other did not seem to care about accompanying him—doubtless in the belief that he would in due time hear everything from his partner.   Perhaps too Perk did not happen to have just as much confidence in the hired guard as Jack seemed to feel.   The remembrance of that burned garage and badly injured Pitcairn Mailwing crate may have still remained too fresh in his memory to let him recklessly abandon their ship in the midst of a strange airport.

Jack was just as well pleased, for he could carry out his business with better results if the talkative Perk were absent although of course Jack would never be guilty of letting his chum know this little fact.

Perk, having eaten a dry snack before they landed, was not very hungry and he had told Jack to be sure and get his dinner at some restaurant while in the city, so that part of the day's doings was taken care of nicely.

It was several hours afterwards when Jack showed up again.   Perk could not notice anything about his appearance to suggest that a monkey wrench had been dropped in the machinery of their projected flight, hence he took it for granted Jack must have had a gratifying confab with Mr. Robert Mills Maxwell, to whom he had been directed to apply, a Government official who would be able to give him the latest news concerning the notorious Hawk and his lawless doings up there in the Northwest Territory where the Canadian Mounted Police held sway.

Perk beckoned to his pal to join him, for at the time he happened to be sitting on a bench not far distant from their hangar and had made up his mind the spot would be an admirable one for them to have their little council of war, after Jack had detailed his adventures in the city.

"How's things?" Perk started in by asking in a general way.

"All serene," came the ready answer accompanied by a nod. "I spent nearly an hour and a half with Mr. Maxwell and found him a most agreeable sort of a gentleman. It was certainly a pleasure to sit and chat with him. He gave me the latest information and just now I'll only say there is to be no change in our program — the whole thing goes through as we figured it." Perk showed signs of sheer pleasure.

"Hot ziggety dog! but I'm right glad to hear that, partner," he remarked eagerly. "I sure do hate to swap hosses when crossin' a stream an' we got things pretty well set up as 'tis. How long will we be stickin' round this Spokane airport, I wonder?"

"Perhaps we may take off in the morning, but a good deal depends on certain things. I may have to see Mr. Maxwell again if he sends out a message by telephone this afternoon. I'm still using my new name, you understand—he thinks it a bright idea, both now and later on when we'll be running across the trail of the man we want most to strike."

"Huh! Mister John Jacob Astorbilt, o' course an' by the same token I'm Gabe Smith, Esq., from the glorious State of Maine an' known as one o' the slickest woods guides goin'. Whoopee! nothin' like layin' it on thick when you're about it. But I want to say that I'll breathe easier after we cut loose from all these strange airports an' strike the open away up in the Canadian bush country."

"Nothing to worry about that I can see, brother," Jack said soothingly, "I can guess what's on your mind and that was a sad sight I admit, seeing such a dandy craft nearly ruined by the fire but I've got a dependable man to watch things here tonight and even if we have a single enemy in Spokane, which I doubt, he'll never get a show down to injure our fine ship."

"Mebbe so Jack, an' already I feel a bit more confidence in the chap you picked up. I've been chattin' with him—he's a married man with a wife an' two kids. More than that I've learned he was raised in that great old State o' Maine an' not fifty miles, as the crow flies, away from the place where I fust saw daylight. Guess now he's okay. We both seem to have knowed a number o' boys an' that kinder makes it feel like we'd been neighbors. Yep, I guess Ike Hobbs is on the square. Mebbe now I might take a notion to run in with you this afternoon, so's to get some eats an' see a picture—been an age since I had a chance to enjoy myself laughin' at one o' them comics on the screen. How 'bout the place you took dinner at—good enough to stand an encore, buddy?"

That was the real Perk all over again — food appealed to him as regularly as the hour rolled around three times a day, and seven days in the week. Jack laughed to hear his comment, and went on to reassure him.

"Plenty good I reckon, Perk old boy and I'll take pleasure in steering you around to the place this evening. Be sure to have your appetite along for they've got a menu almost a yard long so you can have a wide choice."

"Oh! you c'n depend on me carryin' my appetite wherever I wander — jest can't nohow get away from it—haunts me like my shadow an' has ever since I c'n remember. They tells me I never could get filled up like most kids, no matter how they chucked it into me. Any real particular news come your way down thar in town, Jack?"

"A little that was interesting, I'd call it," came

the reply, "although it may be we'll never be called upon to handle the proposition but Mr. Maxwell did seem to be a heap interested in the game and I sure enough promised to help him out, if we chanced to run smack into one of those mule trains."

"What's that, buddy? Je-ru-sa-lem crickets! an' do we expect to try an' rustle stolen mules this time? Wall, I never 'spected the time'd come when I'd be a mule wrangler o' all things!"

"Hold everything and go slow about making up your mind," warned Jack, visibly amused by Perk's evident floundering, "this doesn't happen to have anything to do with mule punchers or even rustlers. It's only a little possible side-line that might happen to develop and of which Mr. Maxwell would have to be advised should we strike pay dirt—that's all, Perk."

"In that case," admitted the now reconciled Perk, "mebbe I might stand for even mules in my itemary or whatever it is I'm aimin' to say. I seen the stubborn critters do some mighty fine work over there in France—mules that came all the way from Missouri in the bargain. But whatever can it be mules has got to do with coaxin' us to turn aside from our main trail, I'd like to know?"

"Just what I'm going to tell you, if you give

me half a chance, brother," explained Jack.
"Here's a little clipping that will explain the
whole thing that's got Mr. Maxwell keyed up to
a high pitch," and he passed a strip taken from
a newspaper to the now deeply interested Perk.

CHAPTER XIII

OVER THE MOUNTAIN TRAILS

This then was what the deeply interested Perk read as he sat there on the isolated bench at the Spokane flying field and it can easily be understood the startling information he soaked in thrilled him to the core:

"The Government agents have been informed of what they suspect will prove to be a gigantic conspiracy to smuggle liquor in immense quantities across the border from Canada into this territory, carried out in an original manner never before attempted and which has thus far met with unqualified success.

"This couspiracy, it is believed, has resulted in bringing many thousands of dollars worth of rum over the line, which has been distributed among the numerous cities of our northwestern country. Several rum rings have, from all accounts, been using pack trains, often well camouflaged, in order to avoid contact with customs officers who might be abroad watching for undesirables.

"These clever smugglers, it appears, adopted numerous devices to hide the long lines of plodding, liquor-laden animals and at times it is claimed they have even driven the mules over United States forestry service trails.

"So systematized are the wide-spread operations of the rum rings said to be that a "traffic manager" has been employed to route the many pack trains from Canada to secluded places opposite the sparsely settled and mountainous Okanogan country in north central Washington.

"Further accounts say that the Pacific manager also watches the weather and when it snows sends white mules along the trails, the animals blending with the whiteness of the landscape. When the ground is bare—bay animals carry the liquor.

"An old time packer who knows how to use the "diamond hitch" in strapping pouchlike containers onto the animals' backs it is claimed is employed to load the mules.

"Heavily armed guards accompany the liquor trains to prevent hijackers from stealing the packs. Whisky and wines are being transported over the winding trails, and upon arrival at the liquor depot all goods smuggled over the border are loaded into automobiles for transportation into many cities throughout the Northwest."

"Well, what do you think of that for a corking dodge?" asked Jack when he saw that his companion had gone through the entire clipping.

Perk shrugged his shoulders quaintly in a way that stood for a good many words, but he only said:

"Gosh amighty! but don't it beat all how some men'll go to such heaps o' trouble jest to make a livin', taking all sorts o' chances to get plugged with hot lead or grabbed up and sent to the pen for a spell?"

"It's the day for reckless engineering, declared Jack soberly enough, with a gold mine always just ahead of the risky scheme. I've heard of some queer games being tried out in connection with the smuggling racket but up to now never had a whisper of anything like the mule pack-train steer."

"Huh! and do you reckon there's any truth in what this paper says or did it jest boil up in the brain o' one o' them reporters, eh Jack ol' hoss?"

"That's what's bothering Mr. Maxwell, it happens," returned the other composedly. "You see, he's responsible to Uncle Sam for keeping things in decent order up here in Oregon and Washington and if such rackets as this can be put through right under his nose, it's bound to get him in bad with the Government. That accounts for him asking me to send him word if we chanced to learn anything worth while about these so-called mule pack-trains, since it would be of some assistance in helping him stamp out the trick."

"Course then partner," went on the eager Perk, "you told the gent we'd be on'y too glad to lend a helpin' hand 'cause to be sure he a'ready knows we're connected with the Secret Service an' runnin' in the same class as he does?"

"That's about the gist of what I told him, Perk and that if the opportunity came our way we'd even go to a lot of trouble so as to help him out. To be sure there might be one chance in ten for us to pick up any worth-while clue but that's dependent on little Lady Luck, as I've heard you say many a time when we were almost muzzled with uncertainty and looking for a lead."

"I'm bound to say the further I get to figgerin' 'bout this queer racket, Jack, the more I like it. Think o' glimpsin' a long string o' mules up in them mountain passes, streamin' along jest like a desert caravan across there in Africa. I've always wanted to lamp such a picture.

Evidently Perk was all keyed up to do everything in his power to lend a helping hand to the Government representative in Spokane of whom Jack had said so many nice things.

He soon settled down after they had lost all trace of the city in the mining sector of the Northwest and proceeded first of all to carry out his accustomed duties with regard to the ship and then when he had time on his hands to begin using his glasses.

It was well worth the trivial effort it cost, that grand view of the mountainous section of country over which they were passing. Here and there Perk could spy little lakes of clear water nestling in secluded valleys or basins and from his elevated position as observer, looking very much like gems in a bold setting.

"Like as not," Perk was telling himself as he looked longingly down on a particularly lovely little sheltered sheet of water, "no white man has ever yanked a gay old trout out o' that lake up to this day! Gee whiz! what wouldn't I give to be settled down alongside that 'ere pond a'flippin' my gang o' flies out over that water an' playin' a three-pound speckled beaut! But no sech luck I kinder guess—not this trip anyway."

They were soon drawing closer to where Jack told him the International Boundary between the States and Canada lay. Of course they would not be apt to know just when they crossed over, since there would be nothing to mark the actual dividing line as happened in Europe where every country is so jealous of the others that each road is guarded, with passports having to be shown and stamped.

His interest grew with their further advance for he could not help remembering what Jack had said concerning those bold international smugglers who were supposed to be continually crossing over from the north with their mule packs laden heavily with the forbidden beverage that was in such great demand among certain circles of law-scoffers.

"Say, mebbe now," Perk told himself at one time—for he had the bad habit of communing with himself on occasion and even seemed to take considerable pleasure in so doing — "I wouldn't be tickled some if on'y I happened to glimpse one of them caravans pullin' through a twistin' mountain trail like I c'n see right down yonder this very minute! An' wouldn't it gimme a heap o' pleasure to swoop down so's to drop a few o' them tear bombs like I did when we blew up the fightin' rum-smugglers and the hijackers that meant to take away their cargo the time we were doin' our huntin' on the gulf coast o' Florida!"*

---

*See *Eagles of the Sky.*

He laughed softly at the recollection of what must have been a pretty stirring piece of action, to judge from what Perk was saying. Then he applied himself with renewed energy to his task of watching that winding mountain trail that vanished again and again, only to bob up shortly afterwards.

"Hugh! somethin' seems to tell me that 'ere must be a well traveled trail an' leadin' down from the north in the bargain," Perk went on to remark as if deeply interested. "I cal'late one o' them 'ere pack mule trains might bob up along that path, if thar's any truth in the stories goin' around and keepin' Mister Robert Mills Maxwell awake nights. It'd be a shame if we missed connections when I know Jack'd give a heap jest to set eyes on the show. Too bad that we'll be losin' all our chances right soon when we strike off to the west. Can you tie it for keepin' a poor feller's nerves all on edge?"

A few minutes afterwards Perk might have been seen to suddenly become rigid, centering his attention on a certain point ahead as though something had caught his strained vision that kept his eyes glued fast.

Jack, intent on his own thoughts and watching his dials with the fidelity of an air pilot who believed in the slogan of safety first, had not become aware of Perk's peocuppied condition so that it gave him something of a little thrill when he felt the other nudge him in the ribs and remark with his peculiar drawl:

"Hot ziggetty dog, partner! **Did I hear you say** *mules?*"

CHAPTER XIV

THE BOOTLEG PACK-MULE TRAIN

"What's up?" demanded Jack as if he could surmise from his companion's peculiar question that Perk had made a pleasing discovery of some kind.

"Lady Luck's gone an' picked us out again to play us for favorites, ol' hoss," Perk told him, at the same time half rising in his eagerness to point out something far ahead.

Jack possessed very good eyesight and as the sun chanced to favor him just then he could manage to make out a snake-like line of small objects that appeared to be moving slowly along in zigzag fashion, evidently following a crooked mountain trail that wound upwards toward the peak of the divide.

"So, that's one of them, is it?" Jack burst out, himself a bit thrilled by the spectacle after having heard so much concerning the pack-mule trains said to have been adopted by the venturesome souls engaged in smuggling operations across the Canadian border.

"With the glass here, Jack, I c'n make 'em out

all to the good," declared the excited Perk — "a fairly big caravan in the bargain, the mules loaded for keeps an' toilin' along jest like they do down in Mexico whar motor cars ain't so plentiful or cheap. Whee! what a sight for sore eyes that is, buddy! Seems like you'll have somethin' to wire Mister Maxwell after all. Nothin' o' a newspaper yarn 'bout *that* bunch, let me tell the world. Must be all o' twenty animals in that string with several boobs mounted on hosses an' armed in the bargain, 'cause I c'n see the sun glintin' from guns they're holdin' as they ride ahead o' the line an' in the rear to boot."

"That goes with the rest of the story, Perk," said Jack as he started toward a lower altitude as though wishing to secure a better view of the moving cavalcade in order to make assurance doubly certain. "You remember we read in that clipping how they carried an armed guard along to defend the caravan in case it was held up by a bunch of hijackers. Queer how these law-breakers make war on each other in cities, the wilderness, and even along the salt water coasts."

"Huh! got to be a part o' the game these days," grunted wise Perk, "jest like the fish-hawk drops down with a rush, grabs up a fat fish from the lake or lagoon and in turn is robbed by the lordly eagle. I kinder guess now that's about where they got the idea o' hijackin'—snatched a leaf from Nature in fact. But say, what are we goin' to do 'bout this thing—why do you strike down closer, I want to know, Jack?"

"We ought to get a better look in, for one thing," he was informed, "and if you could only work that little camera of mine once or twice so as pick up to a telltale picture of the caravan, it would be the finest evidence we could send by mail to Mr. Maxwell!"

"Glory! that's a great scheme, boy—watch my smoke! I'm some photographer when it comes right down to brass tacks an' I'll prove it by gettin' you the smartest pictur goin' an' that's no lie either."

Perk seemed to know just where everything aboard the big ship could be laid hold of in what he would call jig-time for almost as he spoke he was clutching the small but excellent camera that Jack owned, he being something of a crank along that particular line.

"I'm meaning to swing around once or twice while lowering the ship," he explained to his companion so that Perk might not waste a single cartridge of film in taking a snapshot prematurely, with distance as a handicap.

"Go to it, partner," sang out his mate quite merrily, "I'll do my little bit when you gimme the word. Got her all fixed up for distance an' the sun happens to be jest right—say, ain't that a sweet sight, though with them mules cavortin' like they might be scared by such a monster bird sailin' over their stupid ol' heads? An' see the guards swingin' around, shakin' them guns at us like they meant to shoo us off by lookin' fe-ro-cious! Zowie! but this is a heap int'restin' I'm sayin', eh Jack?"

"I bet you!" came the short answer, Jack being so taken up with staring at the greatly disturbed pack-train under the swinging airship that he could not find time for further words just then.

Not so loquacious Perk who never knew when to hold his breath since he was peculiarly gifted along that line and could work as well as gabble at the same time.

"Seems like they jest don't know what to think 'bout seein' an airship sailin' over their heads," he went on to say aloud, "an' I kinder guess now some o' them begin to smell a mouse. Think things ain't goin' to run so slick and greased as they've been doin' right along. Another dip like that, buddy, ought to fetch me close enough to get the snap on the bloomin' bunch."

There he held up—for a brief interval. The fact was Perk had not run out of breath but was only so intensely occupied with trying to fix his little camera so that the lens would take in the whole of the lagging mule-pack train that he forgot to keep on speaking.

Really it did seem as though some kindly fortune had conspired to afford all possible assistance in order to successfully carry out this little racket on the part of Perk. Just as his waiting finger pressed the button the entire cavalcade came to a sudden stop. Indeed, if the actors, both two-legged and four-hoofed had intended to make a grand-stand play to the galleries they could hardly have bettered the conditions.

Perk did not stop at his first exposure but with a commendable rapidity turned on another portion of the reel and once again pressed the button, after which he burst into a roar of ecstatic delight.

"Got it that time boys, sure thing an' I bet you all looked pretty for the set-up. Hoopla! Jack, that was a great snap you gave me an' chances are, Mister—er, hey, what's this mean?"

He bellowed the last few words and with a very good reason for something had come to pass that Perk had not reckoned on as part of the program. There was the sudden rattle of firearms from below and—the motor having ceased functioning while Jack continued his smooth dive—all around them could be heard a strange hurtling, hissing sound which an old experienced war veteran like Perk instantly knew must be made by savagely menacing bullets passing in close juxtaposition to their ship.

Then Jack had the situation in hand again as he pulled the stick back against his chest and with a shrill rat-tat-tat they were once more shooting at an upward slant through space, Jack putting his craft through all sorts of angles in hopes of further causing the sharpshooters to miss connection.

Perk had instantly dropped the camera, though luckily it did not go over the side as might have happened, Jack knew his mate was making a swift sweep with his hand and could give a fairly shrewd guess what his object might be, knowing Perk's combative disposition as well as he did.

The worst of the danger was really past, since they had made such a speedy getaway after that first lunge. Anxious to hold the impulsive one in check, since nothing was to be gained from further aggravating the rum-runners, he continued to keep up that eccentric motion until they had climbed sufficiently to prevent Perk from starting hostilities on their side.

"Swing around and let's go down once more

partner," implored Perk, keenly disappointed because his golden opportunity had given him the slip.

"Oh! I reckon it isn't worth while," replied Jack evenly as though not nearly so stirred up as his chum seemed to be and as he thus spoke kept on going, with the ship headed due northwest by north.

"But—see here Jack, you don't mean to let 'em have the merry ha ha on us, I sure hope? Why, it's got my blood het up to nigh the boilin' point right now. On'y a little slip so I c'n reach the blamed bunch with my machine-gun. For ol' times' sake I'd like to pepper that crowd good an hard! The nerve o' 'em, dustin' us with that shower o' lead! Might have bust our biler an' then where'd we been, tell me? Jest one swoop an' I'll be satisfied. I could get in a dozen shots before they'd have time to crawl under their mules."

But Jack was obdurate to his wild entreaties.

"No use Perk," he told the other through means of the handy ear-phone apparatus. "They failed to do us any damage, though their intentions were plain enough and remember, 'he who laughs last laughs best'. If your snapshot turns out fairly decent it's bound to put a lot of those dangerous guys in the soup when Mr.

Maxwell fits out a bunch of revenue men to round them up. In other words, brother, because of our little job today the chances are we've put the kibosh on this bootleg mule-train racket and for keeps in the bargain!"

CHAPTER XV

WINGING INTO THE NORTHLAND

Perk was still in a high rage because of their having been subjected to that shower of whistling lead.

"For two cents—if you 'lowed me to do it partner," he boomed with many a shake of his head, "an' swooped down once more, I'd a let loose on them pesky jayhawkers an' rum-runners with my bully o' machine gun. It'd seem jest like ol' times come back agin an' you bet I'd a pickled a few o' the rattlesnake bunch!"

"Remember Perk, we're not up here to pickle anybody. This is only what you might call a little side-show — the big round-up lies further north where we've been given a job to tackle—we're just on our way—that's the whole thing in a nutshell."

As usual Perk soon calmed down, being sensible enough to realize that no injury had been done either their ship or themselves. They had met up with a stirring little adventure and come out of the row with credit which ought to be satisfactory, on their side at least.

"What dye s'pose them yaps think 'bout us flyin' so low down over their heads like we wanted to take a peep at the mule pack train?" he presently asked the one at the stick.

"That's something we can only give a guess at," Jack told him. "They're just naturally suspicious as all lawbreakers are and I reckon right now they're likely comparing notes to try and get a line on our standing."

"Huh! guess now you might mean whether they had anything to fear 'bout our ship or not, eh partner?"

"That's the idea, buddy. Up in this part of the country air craft are a rarity, I should say and they must be a whole lot suspicious after having us dip down as we did. I don't imagine any one saw that you were taking a snapshot of the pack train, for they had no glasses that I noticed."

"Oh! that part worked okay ol' hoss," quickly announced Perk, "I didn't make any show when I snapped the gun off but we sure got 'em guessin' if I know my beans an' I figger I do. If you don't mind mentionin' the fact partner, how do you mean to get in touch with Mister Maxwell so's to let him know what's goin' on up here on these mountain trails?"

"I'll find a way to do that before long," came the confident answer. "Of course, he may not be able to lay a trap for this particular pack-train but they keep on coming, and like as not the next convoy will run up against a snag. Mr. Maxwell I imagine, is a corker of an operator, one who never lets the grass grow under his feet when there's need for quick action. Some fine morning, after we get back from this trip, we'll be apt to read all about how this rum-running business with mules carrying the stuff over the mountains, has been smashed to a powder and all the head men put behind bars."

"Unless I'm away off my guess," further remarked the loquacious Perk — who seemed wound up and just must keep going for so long before cooling off—"that clippin' said somethin' 'bout a warehouse on this side o' the line. Reckon now there's anythin' in that report, Jack?"

"You're a little off the track there, brother," he was told. "No such thing as a warehouse was mentioned. It simply stated that it was believed the pack trains all centered at a certain point where they had big, powerful trucks in waiting to carry the smuggled cases to certain cities where they were in cahoots with the authorities — meaning of course, that the officers sworn to carry out the laws of the country and their own State, are taking graft and closing their eyes to what is going on."

"Huh! nice kettle o' fish when such things c'n

go on with the jails so full now they're turnin' the real criminals out to make room for these pizen snakes in the grass."

"That's none of our business, Perk. We're only a part of the Secret Service layout with our work mapped out for us. When we've shown up with results, that's as far as we've got to consider —let the solons do the rest."

Something in Jack's decisive manner of saying this must have warned the talkative one the matter had been threshed out as far as was needful for the time being and that it would be just as well if they relapsed into silence so as to consider other matters that were really more important.

So Perk clamped on the lid and talked only to himself for a long time afterwards, a sport that generally afforded him considerable joy and satisfaction.

Time passed, with their ship keeping up its swift passage, now close to the tops of outlying ridges and anon passing over valleys so far beneath the voyagers that objects to the naked eye assumed very diminutive proportions.

No further mule pack-trains were sighted but then Jack had considered this fact and had no expectation of meeting up with a second caravan. Because of the existing necessity for guarding the high-priced booze they dealt in, so as to be prepared to resist an encounter with bandits known in the rum racket under the name of hijackers, the expeditions could only be sent off at stated periods and there might not be another for a week or two.

It was all pretty wild country over which they swept as on the wings of an eagle heading for the breeding places of its species far up toward the Arctic Circle and in due time Perk began to weary of staring down at such monotonous pictures.

Once they passed over a railroad and he felt thrilled by the thought that man's ability to invade the most inaccessible regions of the earth had put a bit and bridle into the mouth of even so wild a horse as such a land could be compared to in the mind of a visionary fellow like Perk.

On they went, still penetrating deeper into the mysterious northland and heading for that isolated post of the Canadian Mounted Police that was said to be at the extreme edge of the uninhabited stretch lying south of those desolate barrens touching on the Arctic regions where, according to Perk's way of describing things, might be found the jumping-off place that gradually fades away into the near Polar ice-cap.

It was as Jack had learned, a great country for pelts and with signs of gold cropping out of the soil in a myriad of places. The only living hu-

man beings likely to be met with would be lone
trappers running lines of traps in the dreadful
winter season, occasional daring prospectors and
stray Indian villagers during the summer when
they carried on their annual hunt for meat to be
cured for winter use.

Here too, might be found in secret hideouts
more than a few fugitives from justice—men
who had fled from the long arm of the law and
lived the lives of hermits, their hand against all
others and compelled by necessity to play the
part of desperadoes.

Such a dominating character as the Hawk
would not be long amidst such surroundings before he gathered to his standard a select number
of like bold spirits. These would be only too
willing to follow him in his raids on the stores of
isolated fur-takers, white or red, it mattered not,
since all men looked alike in their eyes or making occasional more ambitious forays upon some
outpost and trading center of the great Hudson
Bay Company.

Even the Mounties it seemed had thus far
been baffled in all their efforts to break up this
powerful and elusive corporation of evildoers, so
cleverly handled were the go-getters under the
Hawk that they had a rare faculty for slipping
out of any trap set for them, just as the Irish-

man's flea never was where he jabbed his finger down.

It tickled Perk's vanity considerably to think a problem that had so long been too much of a knotty one to be solved by those wonderfully smart members of the Mounties had now, after a fashion, been transferred to the shoulders of himself and comrade—that the stern resolution on the part of the Government at Washington to recapture the criminal who had given the penitentiary at Leavenworth French leave had so worked out as to form a sort of partnership between the Secret Service and the constabulary of the Great Northwest country.

Having himself served in the ranks with some of those Mounties, it was puzzling Perk tremendously as to just how his former comrades had fallen down on the job of bringing in the Hawk. He had always believed that they never failed to get their man, sooner or later, being ready to follow him to the Pole itself if necessary and to ease his worried mind of this strain he now, as usual, turned his batteries on Jack once more.

CHAPTER XVI

BAFFLED BY HEAD WINDS

During the last hour or two their progress had not been so entirely satisfactory as they might have wished, on account of head winds that held them back more or less. This, however, did not give Jack the slightest uneasiness for as he so often told his more impatient companion, they were in no haste and that more battles were won by slow resistless pressure than by mere swiftness, as history would testify.

"Jack," observed Perk when he felt in dire need of receiving information on the special subject that was giving him distress, "c'n you put me wise jest how come the Mounties ain't never yet been able to grab this Hawk, as they call him—the feller we've set out to yank off'n his high perch? From what I know 'bout the boys, thar didn't ever come along any problem they couldn't straighten out. It's a sorter slogan, as you might call it, with the Mounties that once they sets off on the track o' a marked man he's goin' to be fetched in, no matter how far he runs or how many pals he's got to back him up. I'm

sure bothered a heap to know what's happened
to the force if they've fallen down on this here
job."

Jack made light of the matter, however.

"Nothing queer about that, partner," he told
the mourning Perk. "Your friends the Mounties are only human after all. It's true they've
the reputation of always getting their man but
you must take that with a grain of salt, Perk.
There must have been occasions—rare enough
I'll grant you—when in spite of all they could
do their game got away or else kept on giving
them the slip until perhaps he got into a row
with some of his own gang and was wiped out."

"Yeah! that does seem reasonable I own up, ol'
hoss," Perk admitted a bit against his will as the
other could understand, "but this critter keeps
on thumbin' his nose at 'em and playin' hob with
decent folks' affairs. Don't seem as if the boys
might be keepin' up with the reputation they had
when I chanced to be playin' in their backyard."

"I wouldn't say that if I were you, Perk,"
remonstrated Jack, "we've got to consider that
lots of changes have come along in the last few
years to alter the conditions. For instance, just
see what we're doing right now, hopping along
so merrily at the rate of two miles a minute with
nobody to hold us up. Suppose the Mounties
were hot on the track of a desperado,—then all

at once they heard a great clatter and saw an airship rising above the pines with two men aboard, one waving his hat at them and making gestures of disdain—what could they do about such a getaway? He could be a thousand miles distant in ten hours and none of them know whether he went south, east or out over the ocean."

"Hot ziggetty dog! I never did think o' that sorter thing, partner," confessed the awakened Perk, knocking his fist gently against his head as if to stir up his sluggish brain so as to grasp the new condition of affairs as presented by his wideawake chum. "Mebbe now the boys ain't dropped back any, it's on'y that the workaday world has gone an' bust up ahead—'less you keep abreast o' these here inventive times you soon git left in the lurch. Airships that c'n run upside-down—radio that c'n span half the world so's a feller hears King George talkin' right over in London—talkin' movies that you could enjoy even with Byrd down down at the Antarctic Polar regions—gosh! it ain't no wonder if the Mounties do once in a great while let their man slip away! We're livin' in too fast an age for old ways to bring in the bacon."

Apparently Perk had plenty to think about since Jack had enlightened him in this fashion, at any rate he asked no further questions but went about his various duties with a thoughtful face.

Now he was making a test to ascertain just how their supply of fuel was holding out and informing the pilot of the result, knowing how this must always be a matter of moment to any one getting so far away from the outskirts of civilization as they were then where they could have scanty hope of adding to their diminishing store in case of near exhaustion.

But on comparing results Perk found no cause for anxiety on this score, since his deductions corresponded with the figures previously obtained by his chum Jack who had a decided flair for making accurate estimates in advance.

Perk made his customary rounds, investigating conditions and with a keen eye seeking the faintest indication of possible faults in the running of the airship.

Then that age-old trouble began to assail him and he realized that he had a most aggravating vacuum that really ought to be attended to if he wished to retain his peace of mind. The sun was as near the zenith and it was high time they had a snack calculated to carry them along until they found a chance to cook a real meal for since they would be apt to settle down with the approach of evening Perk had already made up his mind he would have a genuine camp supper, memories of that recent feast seeming to haunt him most tantalizingly.

Possibly too, the tricky fellow may have had a few little surprises in the way of unusual supplies with which he hoped to bring a happy grin on the face of his comrade—an old scheme with Perk by the way—one word for his pal and two for himself.

Another lovely little lake appeared way down below, making about a score they had glimpsed since starting out on the hop from Spokane that morning, each one presenting some additional novel feature that caused Perk to stare and admire. He even found himself wishing Jack might finally decide to take advantage of the presence of a body of water where they could feel comfortable while the night lasted. Later on Perk figured on suggesting that idea to the pilot for indeed, since ground landing places were so few and far between in that mountainous country, it would seem as though such a policy might be the only one they could adopt.

Jack, when he saw the spread made by his chum, announced himself as ready to assist in making way with the food supply, though he would wait until Perk had taken his toll when he meant to turn the stick over to him for a spell.

This programme was duly carried out and no time lost. Perk compared it to a traveler seated in the diner of a limited express train heading for Los Angeles or New York City.

"But stop and think, brother, how old-fashioned you are right now," Jack told him, his mouth well filled just then with the sandwich he was enjoying. "Why, today they have cross-country airships that carry complete dining outfits with a first-class chef in attendance, also sleeping berths to be made up when night draws close. You'll have to get a move on, buddy, for the procession is already at your heels and threatening to take your number."

Perk grinned and knocked that head of his again.

"Guess you said somethin' that time, partner. These youngsters sure have old chaps like me on the run for keeps. But I got a notion there are a few things the ol' guys c'n still manage an' as long as I'm able I reckon to keep goin', with aviation my chief diet."

"Well," said Perk, "never give up the ship as long as you've got an ounce of steam left in the boiler," and Jack turned his head once more to the supply of dry food and cold coffee that Perk had set out for his attention.

An hour afterwards he insisted on taking the controls once more. Perk, in hopes that he might be thinking of dropping down when some tempting lake came in sight, said nothing, though figuring on broaching the subject presently when the sun sank a little further toward the western horizon.

The obstreperous head wind that had delayed them for so long still hung on, though very likely it would die out at sunset. If they had failed to cover all the ground such a run might have given them, at least they were far advanced on their way.

Then something happened, for suddenly Perk missed the steady roar of the motor and on looking up discovered the ship was pointing down as though in a direct glide. His first belief was that, just as he had hoped, Jack was bent on taking advantage of an opportunity to drop down on some lake ahead.

"Goin' to use the pontoons again, eh partner?" he called out as if to show his companion he himself had been figuring on the chances of doing that thing when to his amazement he heard Jack saying in a steady voice:

"Case of necessity—got to make a dead-stick landing—hold yourself steady now, Perk, and leave it to me!"

CHAPTER XVII

JACK'S DEAD STICK LANDING

Perk proved game all right—not the least bit flustrated or upset but just took it as a matter of course—an incident likely to bob up in the checkered life of any airman and with which doubtless he had himself been acquainted in days that were long since gone.

He did, however glance swiftly ahead toward the spot where in all probability, barring further accidents, the amphibian would be apt to make contact.

"Gee whiz! what born luck that guy does have!" was what flashed through his brain for what did he see before him but a sheet of water, one of those lovely little lakes over which they had passed again and again and which at all times had excited both his curiosity and his envy.

"Oh! if *on'y* he c'n make it," Perk kept saying half to himself and perhaps hardly conscious of his eagerness in the matter, for only too well did he know how lessened their chances of avoiding a bad crash would be if they could hit that water harbor when they struck on a slant.

It was a critical moment for the success or failure of the entire expedition, for even though neither of them were killed outright they might be injured so seriously that the object of the flight must sink into oblivion in comparison with the task of getting the wounded one to a doctor.

Then in addition to those chances, what if their ship became totally disabled? At that distance from civilization it would be next to impossible for it to be salvaged and in consequence the costly amphibian would prove a total loss.

No wonder then, that for the brief few seconds previous to their pontoons striking, both of the chums found their hearts ceasing to beat in so far as their knowledge told them—at any rate, they held their breath in anticipation of the worst.

To be sure there was an enormous amount of splashing as though some ancient rock had chosen to alight in that little mountain lake. Once Perk was sure they must capsize and lose everything but just in the nick of time Jack cleverly shifted his position and this seemed to right the boat.

Jack had done wonderfully, considering the handicap under which he labored. The spot where they struck was about two-thirds across the lake so that it turned out they had plenty of room to glide ahead after the first rude shock was over.

The two occupants of the cabin boat turned, as if by some instinct, to grin at each other. No one, to observe their apparent indifference, would have dreamed what a close shave they had just encountered for landing with the stick absolutely inert is not the nicest thing in the world and has caused more than a few bad crashes in which life was snuffed out or at least sadly battered.

"Huh! couldn't a done it any better myself," remarked Perk, making a wry face as though to tell his pal to interpret those words in the light of a joke which circumstances did not bother Jack in the least. He had a high estimation of his comrade's abilities and pluck and rather fancied Perk might be a bit better than himself in some things connected with flying. No ace is such a complete master of his calling that he has no rival worthy of the name.

"Well, we're down, seems like," ventured Perk after taking a survey all around the wonderful little body of sparkling icy water where they had so miraculously dropped from near the clouds.

"That part is attended to, and sooner than I had figured," stated Jack with a shrug of his shoulders that spoke volumes.

"Say, was you meanin' to pick out one o' these lakes for a campin' place tonight, eh, ol' hoss?" demanded Perk, "'cause I had it all fixed to coax you to do that thing. Kinder hankerin' some for a layout ashore, where we c'n have a cookin' fire, an' stretch our legs as we feel like."

Jack nodded in the affirmative.

"I had that all arranged in my mind, partner," he admitted, "but from the way things turned out, the ship didn't mean to wait on my pleasure. You'd think she had fallen in love with this special body of water, from the hurry she was in to make it. Just the same we got off mighty lucky, boy."

"Sure did, Jack, and now the next question is, can we hop off from here when the right time comes along?"

"No trouble about that, I reckon," replied Jack after a quick glance around. "These steep mountains shut things in kind of tight but just remember, brother, that these are not the old days, when ships needed a half mile down-grade runway so's to get up enough speed to be lifted from the ground and the same goes for an amphibian or seaplane."

"Hot ziggetty dog! guess you must mean the notched wings, eh, partner?" blurted out Perk.

"Just so, and I calculate I can take her out of this hole in the mountains as slick as grease,—

when we're ready to get busy," was Jack's superbly confident declaration, said not as a boast, but with the calm assurance of one who knew what he was talking about.

"Wonder what did ail the boat to make that stick go dead so you couldn't get a wiggle outen it?" Perk mused as though something brought his thoughts suddenly around to the fact that thus far neither of them had any thorough knowledge concerning this cause of the sudden forced landing.

"We'll get around to that right away," the other told him, "but even if we should learn what we want to know, and must find out, there'd be no reason for us to climb out of this snug nest this afternoon that I can see."

"Bully for you, Jack, ol' hoss, I was jest hopin' that'd be our programme. Kinder took a likin' for these sweet little lakes an' wouldn't mind spendin' a night on the bank o' this one. Might somethin' turn up to give us a whirl—never c'n tell, I guess, what's goin' on away off here in the wilds, where two-legged critters are as scarce as hens' teeth."

That was the same old Perk showing his deep-seated love for action. It had grown upon him over across the big water, at the time he was with the balloon corps in France, and became a part of his very nature ever since so that he could not keep from sighing for a change whenever stagnation set in.

Accordingly Jack led the way and they began a minute examination of the stalled motor. Both of them were more or less proficient in all matters connected with airplane engines, although it seemed as though a new species of trouble was springing up every little while, requiring fresh study in order to master the problem.

A whole hour was spent in checking things up before Jack discovered what ailed the hitherto perfect mechanism in which he had come to place the most implicit confidence. He proceeded to show Perk what he had thus found out and to demonstrate the surest way to correct the fault.

"After all, that's one on me," Perk soon frankly admitted, "but I kinder guess you've solved the riddle, ol' hoss. Next thing to find out is whether we c'n fix it out here so far from everything."

"No great trouble about that, partner," said Jack. "You play a while and let me dig around— not any too much room for two guys to work in and fact is I won't need any help—if I do I'll call you."

"Okay with me, Jack, since our left wing jest tips the shore I guess I'll step off an' have a look around. Everything looks quiet enough, so mebbe there'll be no need o' me luggin' that heavy machine-gun along."

"Suit yourself about that, partner," remarked Jack in an absent-minded way, as though his thoughts were pretty much taken up with the job he had on hand.

So Perk went ashore and began to prowl around, that being one of his customary amusements when the opportunity presented itself. He walked here and there so as to get various glimpses of the glorious sheet of water—bent down and drank his fill, remarking upon its ice-cold character, coming as it did from melting snow on the caps of near-by mountains or possibly from some hidden glacier that dated back many centuries.

All around him was a dead silence, broken from time to time by a chinking sound, made as he knew, by Jack laboring at the stubborn motor.

"Huh! seems like this might be a dead country away up here," Perk told himself as he continued to climb around among the masses of huge rocks that in the centuries past must have rolled down the abrupt slopes. "Not a hoof or a claw movin', when I kinder spected to glimpse a bear mebbe or it might be a panther, p'raps a Canada lynx."

"Hey Perk!" he heard Jack calling and then came the loud staccato notes of the motor, sound ing as sweet music in Perk's ears.

CHAPTER XVIII

AROUND THE CAMPFIRE

The rejuvenated motor continued to sing most merrily as Perk hastened to cover the back trail leading to the ship nesting upon the quiet lake.

"Huh! I jest knew Jack could get the hang o' things," he told himself in high glee, "makes a big clatter I'll tell the world, but after you've been forced to drop down agin your will, they ain't nuthin' in natur so sweet as the drummin' o' a ship's motor. Some fine day mebbe we'll have the good luck to be runnin' a boat with twin motors, so if one kicks off the duplicate c'n carry on."

After he joined his mate and duly examined what Jack had done, the sound of the beating motor ceased since there was no need of wasting any more juice to celebrate the happy occasion.

"That trouble will never happen again with me," Jack was saying with grim earnestness. "I know just how it must have come about and expect to put the kibosh on any repetition."

"Jest as you've said to me many a time, partner," Perk spoke up, "an ounce o' prevention's

a heap better'n a pound o' cure. Learnin' somethin' new ev'ry day, seems like, but it's okay if
on'y you keep the same trick from springin' up
again an' gettin' your goat."

They took things easy and lay around for another hour and more. Jack, as usual, consulted
his chart and did some figuring. Perk, quite
content to let the Chief do most of the planning,
amused himself in various ways, as was his habit
when they were not flying. Puttering with this
little thing, poking around the stores as if to
figure just how many more meals would exhaust
what he had laid in so bountifully and bring
them near starvation and tiring at length of this
sort of thing he lapsed into inaction, puffing at his
beloved pipe and indulging possibly in day-
dreams.

Once Jack chanced to turn an inquiring eye in
his direction to see him nodding his head and
counting his fingers, as though adding up some
score.

"At it again, I bet a cookey," Jack thereupon
told himself, holding back the casual remark he
had intended making, "browsing on that same
old game of trying to remember a name by going
over the whole alphabet again and again. Poor
old Perk, how that defective memory does bother
him. He'll get no peace of mind until he happens to strike what he's fishing for and since I

never did hear the boy's full name mentioned I just can't help him a mite."

Jack had guessed aright, for just then Perk was saying to himself in a low but earnest tone, something of the old formula:

"Sufferin' cats! it sure began with an R I bet my boots! Randolph, no, don't jest sound right to my ear—Ratcliff, Randall, Ratterman—strikes me it ended in man—Rodman—hang the luck, what the devil *is* the matter with my think-box? Did you ever know sech a tantalizin' mess—just openin' my trap to say it out loud when before I could get the right word out it slipped me like a wet cake o' soap on the bath-room floor when you set a foot on it. I'm sure hoodooed for keeps, an' it's no good."

By this time the afternoon was wearing away and before long night would be putting a dark blanket over the deep notch in the mountains. Perk suddenly came out of his fit of abstraction to remark cheerily:

"Guess now it's 'bout time I got busy ashore, an' started that 'ere fire. I gathered some fire-wood ready an' it ain't goin' to take much time to get supper goin'."

Accordingly he began to fill his arms with the things previously set aside, consisting for the most part of food, coffee pot, skillet and last but not least, the dependable machine-gun with which a provident Government had fitted out its flying detective squad when starting them on their way to rounding up lawbreakers who were in many instances taking to the air.

"Call me when you're ready or need any help, brother," Jack told him, he being still engaged in his extensive figuring and marking places on his handy little chart, as though mapping out his campaign as well as such a thing was possible.

Perk had his blaze going in almost record time, for he was an adept at fire-building. Later on, from the delicious odors that came stealing to his olfactories, Jack knew that supper was on the way.

Having by then finished his work, he laid things aside and for the next ten minutes watched the busy one on shore at his pleasing task. It was certainly a picture that was bound to arise again and again in Jack's mind. The star-studded heavens against which towering mountain peaks were outlined, the lapping of little wavelets on the shore where there chanced to be a narrow strip of sandy beach, the neighboring small bunch of pines through which an evening breeze was sighing as if playing Nature's Eolian harp in a lullaby for the lately departed day, the rocky shore line, bordering that limpid gem of a lake where he could hear an occasional trout breaking water—taken in all it was a dream, as Jack told himself more than a few times.

"First call to supper—all that's hungry get goin' while things are hot! I ain't meanin' to wait more'n three shakes o' a lamb's tail 'fore I pitches in. Hi! there, partner, shake a leg!"

The bill of fare may not have been very extensive, but there was an abundance of substantial food and best of all ravenous appetites to be satiated. Perk was as happy as a lark and a dozen times demanded of his comrade if he had ever partaken of anything that tasted better than the slice of ham with the fried eggs to give it the proper caper, after which the coffee came in for his flattery."

"Course I know right well it's awful f'r the cook to praise his own work, but I jest can't help sayin' it's a swell supper, taken in all. Another piece o' fried ham, ol' pard, tho' sorry there ain't no more eggs at all—lucky what I laid by didn't get smashed in the runnin'—which goes to show what a good packer I am—might even get a job with that gang o' mule skinners an' their loads o' moonshine stuff."

Never had Jack seen his chum more joyous as after he had filled up with the appetizing camp supper. He beamed on his mate and only for having laid in such a big supply of grub asserted he'd be tempted to try the fishing as there were surely trout in the lake from their incessant jumping along about sundown when insects skittered about on the surface and mealtime had come for the finny tribes.

In the midst of his chattering Perk suddenly stopped and appeared to be intently listening.

"Well, I guess now," he remarked, grinning, "I was away off my base when I says there ain't nary a wild animal inside o' twenty miles o' this spot 'cause listen to 'em yappin', will you, partner?"

"Wolves I reckon," observed Jack who had also caught the distant sounds.

"Jest what they be," Perk continued triumphantly, "an' sounds to me like they made some sort o' a killin' an' are all het up with the victory. There, died out like snuffin' a candle out, showin' they got started on the grub. Queer what different tastes critters have. Some like their venison raw while others aim to cook it to a turn over red coals an' chaw it while hot. But venison sure is *good* any which way you cook it over a real camp-fire."

Jack saw him lick his lips with his tongue as though even the mention of that chief standby of a hunter's feast made his mouth water. Perk certainly did think a heap of his eats, as he so often frankly admitted.

They heard nothing further from the wolf

pack but at least the circumstance had assured Perk that the rocky mountain sides were not as lacking in big game as he had been convinced earlier in the evening. So too, no doubt he was telling himself that it might pay to keep his gun within reach when the time came for them to hit the hay as he usually termed the act of turning in.

They remained ashore for another hour or so, just on account of the change. The rocks were anything but comfortable as a seat, but Perk managed to find a quantity of moss near by which added to their ease when judiciously applied.

Finally Jack proposed going aboard the ship.

"Me too, Boss!" sang out Perk, "'cause I'm sorter tired an' feel like gettin' rested up. Things look okay to me an' mebbe we'll have a quiet night—if on'y them hungry wolves get filled up an' don't ketch wind o' our bein' in the neighborhood. Hugh! if they know what's good for 'em they'll give this lakeshore a wide berth while me'n my ol' chattergun are on deck."

CHAPTER XIX

PERK GETS A SHOCK

An hour later and both of them were sound asleep, having comfortable let-down cots in the sheltering cabin that were a wonderful improvement over the way they used to double-up in the cramped cockpit of the ship they handled before this fine amphibian was placed in their charge by Uncle Sam.

The night moved on and for some hours nothing occurred to annoy them. Perk had become addicted to waking about once so often and as a rule he used to sit up and yawn as he took a look around.

It may have been an hour or so after midnight when, on thus arousing, he caught a sound that caused him to omit the customary yawn, though he certainly sat up with a jerk and appeared to be listening.

Almost mechanically too, his right hand groped for something alongside his cot and it was his gun he presently pulled up. The sounds he had heard once more broke out—savage,

ominous sounds they were too, undoubtedly pro-
ceeding from one or more wild beasts aroused to
a fighting spirit.

"Huh! bobcats, I'd say, if you asked me, neighbor, an' hoppin' mad in the bargain. Must be
a pair o' 'em an' they ain't mates either. Guess
now two ol' rivals must a met head-on along some
trail an' each is a sassin' t' other, darin' him to
knock a chip off'n his shoulder an' see what he
gets. Gosh amighty! but wouldn't I jest like to
lamp that 'ere duel the wust kind, but I knows
aheap better'n to set out an' spy on 'em. Just as
like as not they'd forget all their mad agin' each
other an' set on me for keeps. Thar they go agin,
licketty-split, snarlin', screechin' and scrappin'
for all that's out. I'm tellin' the wide world the
hair's sure flyin' in big patches while *that* cater-
waulin' keeps grindin' out."

It kept Perk sitting there fully ten minutes
before finally dying out nor did he ever know
whether one or both quarreling creatures had
been extinguished, like the famous cats of Kil-
kenny, each of which thought "there was one cat
too many."

"Some circus, b'lieve me," Perk told himself,
with many a chuckle, for he had been vastly
amused and entertained by that aggregation of
furious sounds, "but it's okay with me so long's

they scrap 'mong themselves an' leave us alone. I ain't lost no kitty as I know of, an' there's some more sleep I c'n make use of if they put the brakes on their whoopin' things up."

With that he snuggled down once more and forgot all his troubles for the balance of the night. If there were any further ancient feuds still to be settled among the old-time inhabitants of that section, Perk was unaware of the slaughter for he did not open his eyes until the first peep of dawn announced the coming of another day.

Jack still slept, it would seem, for he lay there like a mummy while Perk proceeded to crawl out and get into his clothes with the full intention of slipping ashore, reviving the fire and starting to prepare breakfast. Apparently his enormous supper of the previous evening must have digested and that awful vacuum he detested so much was already calling for help.

He chanced to have a sore toe that gave him a painful twitch every little while and not feeling disposed to tramp around collecting fuel until he had remedied this physical distress, he sat down to pull off his footgear and fasten a little wad of cotton between the offending member and its neighbor.

Once while thus busily engaged Perk imagined he caught a slight thud, as of something striking a root or fallen branch. He raised his head to listen, with those ravenous timber wolves flashing into his mind but then everything seemed nice and quiet again so that believing he had only imagined he heard suspicious sounds he once more bent down to complete his little task.

Then, without hardly any warning, there suddenly burst forth the most diabolical sound Perk had ever heard in all his life. Something similar to the braying of army mules over in France, he thought.

Perk probably felt his blood run cold, for that frightful racket was not more than twenty feet distant. Wildly he stared, expecting to see some savage beast, perhaps with the stripes of a real jungle tiger, come leaping from behind the adjacent rock heaps and make directly for him, unarmed as he was.

Regaining the use of his limbs Perk turned tail and made for the friendly left wing of the ship, taking huge jumps and anticipating that some supple body was apt to land on his back despite his haste.

Jack was there in full sight and worse luck, he did not even seem to have thought to snatch up the handy gun when that frightful roar echoed and re-echoed up and down hill in the valley of the silver lake.

"G—et th' gun, quick—tigers, lions, an' nobody knows what not—on the rampage to beat the band, too!"

Jack stared and then seemed to fairly double-up as though to him there might be something worth laughing at in the hurried retreat of his pal.

"He's more scared than you can be, Perk!" he managed to cry out. "See him making off, will you, taking steps that are nearly as long as your own. Watch him shake those new horns of his, as if to tell you he'd be willing to fight it out only his head pieces are so new like, and soft!"

"W-hy—what in tarnation thunder is that big monster, Jack?" gasped the astonished Perk, staring with all his might after the towering beast that was passing out of sight around a vast mound of tumbledown rocks.

"Only a bull moose, partner—he must have heard you make some sound and reckoned it was an old rival of his, which was what made him give that roar. I never ran across a moose up to now, but I know what they can do. If it had been in the Fall of the year, when his horns, just rutting lately, were firm and hard, you'd have had him jumping you mighty quick."

"Wow! he *had* me jumpin' even as it was," confessed honest Perk, deigning now to break into a silly grin since the supposed danger was past and the coast clear. "He's some jim dandy I'd say an' mebbe I wouldn't like to knock a bull moose over. Used to hear about 'em when I was a kid up in Maine and over the line in Canada too (but never met one o' the breed before. Bet you that ol' boy c'n run a blue streak too, once he lets go. Well, since there ain't any tigers at large nor yet a catamount lyin' in ambush, guess I orter go ashore again an' hurry up my fire. Breakfast ready in ten minutes, 'member, Jack ol' hoss."

While working over his fire and starting breakfast Perk must have been sketching in his mind the nerve racking encounter so lately in the spot-light, for once he stopped doing what he was engaged in, to look seriously up at the blue sky where a few floating white clouds had taken on a faint pink blush, showing that the rising sun was not far below the horizon though not scheduled to appear to any one in that deep valley for several hours yet—then he might have been heard holding communion with himself and saying:

"I kinder guess moose steak wouldn't taste so bad but then what's the use o' cryin' over spilt milk? Mister Moose has skipped out an' then Jack wouldn't let me shoot, even if the ol' critter hung around lookin' for trouble. Didn't he say the close season was on with all game that you c'n eat and that the Mounties might get me if I took chances and nailed that big boy? Oh well! I'm all to the good and no tellin' what he might have done to me if we got mixed up in a sure enough scrap."

Breakfast was almost as enjoyable as supper had been —not just wholly so for no one is ever quite so hard pressed by hunger in the early morning as seems to be the case toward close of day when all cares are tossed aside.

Jack did not appear to be in any hurry to leave the scene of their night's bivouac for he puttered around, doing numerous small chores that, according to Perk's mind, could have just as well been postponed to another time without the sky falling.

"Ain't she ready to take the air, Boss?" he finally demanded when he could stand it no longer, whereupon Jack looked up smilingly and nodded.

"Everything's as fine as silk, brother, and since it's getting along, perhaps we'd better be on our way."

"Huh! that's the line o' patter I'm longin' to hear from you, partner," Perk broke out in positive relief. "I'm a bit leery 'bout puttin' in a second night alongside this lake. Might have a twenty-foot anaconda drop down on us while we sat outside an' smoked. Now don't tell me they ain't no sech animal hereabouts, 'cause I know that as well as you do but just the same I'm glad we're goin' to climb outen here pronto."

CHAPTER XX

THE FUR-TRADING STATION

Possibly Perk may have been a little troubled in his mind lest they run up against difficulties when trying to climb out of that tiny valley walled with those titanic mountains massed all around.

His faith in the ability of his comrade to surmount ordinary difficulties and aviation perplexities buoyed him up and he failed to register any outward signs of undue anxiety.

His confidence was well placed for aided by the excellent working of the crate's slotted wings and his knowledge concerning their control, Jack was enabled to start boring up toward the sky almost as soon as the amphibian quitted the placid bosom of the crystal lake.

A few circles and they had risen so that it was possible to see beyond the peaks by which they were surrounded.

"That's the boy—beautifully done, I'll tell the gapin' world—an' what a good feelin' it gives a flyer to know he's on the wing once more after bein' knocked down by a dead-stick swattin' him.

Glad now I snapped off them two pictur's jest when we was leavin' the lake under us."

"Same here partner," chimed in Jack, "for I'll always have a kindly feeling for that little cup of water set in that hole among the mountains like it might be a precious diamond in a platinum ring."

"Huh! I'd like to said that same thing, buddy," Perk told his mate, "on'y it ain't in my blood to spout poetry you see but a feller c'n *feel* it in his heart, mebbe, even when he jest can't say it."

"Which is as true as anything can be," vowed Jack who was well aware of the limitations of his chum and could appreciate his good points, even if in some ways Perk seemed a bit dumb.

They were soon on their course as laid out by the head pilot and making into the north at fair speed. Perk amused himself for some little time in carrying out his accustomed duties, which were numerous and so essential they must not be neglected. Later on Jack, realizing that Perk was no longer moving around with his customary bustle, managed to steal a glance in his direction to discover that the other was snuggled down and seemed to be gazing at something he held in his hand, as though wrestling with a weighty problem.

Jack immediately understood, for the object

at which Perk stared so earnestly happened to be the small photograph he had received from the youngster whom he, Perk, had carried across that queer little bridge made of two ironing-boards when the tenement was burning in Salt Lake City.

He would turn it over so as to read the name written in a female hand on the back—"Adrian, at six years," and then quickly reverse the card as if he hoped to instinctively pronounce the last part of the lad's name that seemed to elude his memory with such disgusting pertinacity.

But apparently even that idea failed to work, for Jack heard no triumphant whoop break from his companion's lips as he felt certain would be the case should he hit what he was after. The old saying, all signs fail in dry weather, was applicable in Perk's case, it seemed. Still, such are the vagaries of the human memory that he was likely to suddenly utter the word he wanted just as he opened his eyes after a nap. It often comes about that way as many persons can testify.

Jack shook his head and grinned, muttering to himself meanwhile:

"Queer how poor old Perk does get so twisted up with names and he's so dogged about it he never will give in till he gets what he's after. Always makes me think of that ad. I used to see in the magazines about some kind of toilet soap. A baby in his little tub stretching out a hand to lay hold of a cake of soap and underneath the words: 'he'll never be happy till he gets it.' That's my pal Perk to a fraction—wish I could give him the high sign but since I never heard the name it's beyond my ken. But anyway it gives him something to play with, like a baby's rattle and how he does hang on to it."

So Perk kept on staring goggle-eyed at that picture, just as if it mattered as much as three cents whether he ever again heard of the boy or his mother, both of whom Jack had somehow made up his mind, were evidently engaged in a search for some missing party who was especially dear to them but whose identity was now, and probably always would be, a complete mystery to the pair who had befriended them on that night of the fire.

"After all," Perk finally said, and Jack could easily catch every word, thanks to the useful ear-phone apparatus they had on, "we did have a fine time o' it—you made the neatest dead-stick landin' I ever seen put through — we had a glorious supper an' a nice night in camp as I might say—glimpsed a' ol' galliwampus o' a big bull-moose on the gallop—it'd jest be complete if on'y I had a decent head on me so's to grab that name—Adrian—Adrian what—shucks?"

Jack did not say a single word lest he start the other to worrying again. It might seem such a trifling matter to any outsider but to Perk it meant that he was growing old—that his memory, never any too good, had taken to going back on him worse than ever.

The further they worked into the north the more uninhabited did the wild region seem to become. Earlier in their flight they were able to occasionally discover an isolated log-cabin marking the lonely home of some venturesome white trapper and when these isolated shelters were still occupied by their owners there would be a column of wood smoke rising above the adjacent timber that made things seem a bit homelike, but for the last hour Perk had not picked up the slightest clue to human existence in all that vast wilderness, though he plied his glasses most industriously in hopes of breaking the spell.

"Must be drawing close to the fur-trading post, I'd reckon, eh partner?" Jack suddenly demanded at which the other nodded vigorously in the affirmative and followed this up by saying emphatically:

"Just what we are ol' hoss. I've seen a number o' things to tell me it's close by here—f'r instance, take a peek at them three cones standin' out there in a triangle off to the west—many a time I've sat an' smoked an' watched the clouds coverin' the lowest peak while on a log in front o' Old Jimmy McGregor's log cabin store. Jest a trifle more to the east, partner, an' chances are we'll be settin' eyes on Frazer's Post inside ten minutes at the most."

That was certainly cheery information for Jack to hear from his companion who was familiar with much of that country from having ridden over the mountain trails when spending several years in the service of the Northwest Mounted Police force.

Perk seemed to be more and more amazed by the fact of their striking the far distant point as though drawn by some magnet, for a minute later he broke loose again.

"There, I 'member that little canyon where the trail runs through — got my first caribou right on that spot—a herd was passin' an' I came on the bunch as they turned a corner. What makes me sit up an' take notice is how we've come all the way up here, hundreds an' hundreds o' miles, straight as a die an' inside o' forty-eight hours, I guess I might call it, when in them days it'd taken me a month anyway to cover the same distance on hossback. They fetches the supplies to the post here by way o' the river an' then by carry. Huh! we're livin' in a great age, strikes me, partner. Now, get ready to take a look-in at the first fur-tradin' station you ever did see 'cause it's jest beyond that little rise with the timber hidin' the fort. Hot ziggetty dog! I never did think I'd be up here in this country again."

Jack also felt a little thrill of expectancy as they sped onward for in another minute or so they should be passing directly over the place Perk had pointed out with such assurance. The trip had thus far been as successful as any one could hope for and their success in finding the needle in a haystack, as Perk had once called their mission, was to be considered a feather in the cap of the pilot.

Then all of a sudden he heard Perk give utterance to a lour cry as of dismay, coupled with astonishment.

"Hey! what's all this mean? Look at that outhouse smoulderin' like it's been burned down inside o' last night! An' that little bunch o' fellers standin' there like they meant to skedaddle at hearin' us comin' with sech a racket! Jack, I tell you somethin's sure happened around these diggin's! Been some sorter o' deviltry afoot an' ten to one that same crazy Hawk's the guy that's broke loose! Mebbe now we jest got here in time to break into the game."

CHAPTER XXI

OLD JIMMY, THE FACTOR

It hardly needed these vigorous words from the startled Perk to tell Jack something unusual was the matter at the trading post. Just as his comrade had declared, some sort of minor building was smouldering, smoke ascending in lazy spirals and occasionally a tiny burst of flame telling where a fresh bit of unburned wood must have fallen to the heat still hanging over the ruins.

Then too, the actions of the parties standing in a clump near the general store and fur repository added to his belief for they did look very much disturbed as if almost tempted to make a break for the shelter of the nearby forest.

That was easily understood, for up to the present time it must have been a rare event for an airplane to come circling over that remote trading post—indeed, perhaps never before had such a thrilling event occurred.

"Jack, you're meanin' to drop down, ain't you?" sang out the worried Perk.

"I reckon to," came the steady answer, "when

you've shown me the open field you said lay close by — that was even enough for a fairly decent landing."

"Why, there it is right now, partner—over on the right, this side o' the tall timber yonder," and Perk thrust out a hand so as to make his meaning quite clear.

"I see it Perk, boy, and must take your word for it we'll have a chance to make contact without a spill. We've got to find out what's been going on around here lately, that's about all there is to it."

"I c'n jest wager it's some dirty work o' that timber wolf, Hawk," asserted the other vigorously, "an' if he's so much as hurt a hair o' Ol' Jimmy McGregor's gray head it's goin' to cost him dear, an' that's no lie either!"

Jack said nothing further, just paid strict attention to his business. He was scanning the rather contracted field so as to figure where he should drop down, with a bit of open space ahead for a short run after hitting the earth.

He had made several circles around the place before coasting earthward as his severe training as a pilot had taught him to do ere making the last dip. In another half minute the wheels had struck and the amphibian was slowing up in its forward thrust.

Both of them hastily detached the 'phones

from their heads for they could see that some of the men, mostly trappers, Jack imagined from their rough dress, were commencing to push toward the spot where the visitor from the clouds lay almost motionless, having withstood such shaking-up as followed the rough landing.

The first thing that Jack noticed was the fact that there was an eager look on several of the leather-like faces of the advancing group. He rather imagined they had been cherishing a wild hope the airship might disgorge several figures in the well-known uniforms of the Mounties and that their recent rough treatment at the hands of the outlaws would soon be avenged.

"Hi! what's been goin' on 'round the post here, boys?" shouted Perk as the small group drew near. "Hello! Birdseye Baker, glad to see you're still on deck—ain't forgot Gabe Perkiser, have you, Oldtimer?"

The tall, stoop-shouldered man with the long hair whom Perk addressed stared hard and then came closer.

"If it ain't Perk hisself!" he explained, to immediately add: "Back on the old job agin, be ye—but why ain't ye in uniform—an' whar be the rest o' the Mounties — we need 'em right smart I'm tellin' ye, boy!"

"Who's been handlin' you rough, brother?" asked Perk sympathetically.

"Cap. Hawk an' his gang. Ain't been gone more'n three hours—stole all my whole season's ketch o' pelts an' robbed Old Jimmy o' his money an' a heap o' stores 'sides. I kinder feel like I'm meanin' to skip out o' this blasted kentry if so be they jest can't nab that wild critter, 'er else make him turn up his toes. What ails the Mounties, I wanter know, when they slip up on a job like this? Don't seem like the days when ye was workin' in the outfit, Gabe Perkiser."

"Hold out a little longer, Birdseye, ol' hoss!" exclaimed Perk jerking off goggles and helmet, "mebbe it'll all come out okay. They's things on the programme that 're goin' to cut a big figger in this game. Just you wait an' see 'fore you cuss the Mounties black an' blue."

Then, as if noting the absence of Old Jimmy the factor, Perk continued, looking anxiously around:

"But where's Jimmy right now, I want to know? 'Taint like him to be stickin' in his coop yonder when strangers come to town!"

"He's on his back, Perk—got into ruction with them bushrangers an' they tore him up somethin' scandalous. Nuthin' real dangerous, get me, but he sure needs the attention o' a doc. I'm told they's sech a man up to the fort name o' Hamilton but we ain't no way o' gettin' word to him in a hurry."

"That's okay, ol' hoss," said Perk quickly, "my boss here, Mister John Jacob Astorbilt is aimin' to strike Fort Laney, hopin' to get some big game shootin' thereabouts. We c'n fetch the sawbones back with us if so be he's still around."

"Good boy, Perk," said the old fur-trapper enthusiastically, "but come in an' see the old man—he'll be right glad to meet up with ye again — often talked 'bout ye when I kim back from my trap line in the Spring."

Perk looked as happy as a schoolboy carrying home *her* books for the first time—showing that after all he was not quite so hard-boiled as he wished to appear and that a little flattery could bring the blushes to his well tanned weather-stained cheeks.

"Let's go, partner," he said motioning to Jack who had been listening to all this talk with increasing interest, since it had more or less to do with the lawless actions of the desperado whom he had been dispatched to bring back to the States so as to be returned to Leavenworth penitentiary, with considerably more time added to his original sentence.

The moment they entered the post they could easily see that something like an eruption must have occurred only recently. Everything was upset as though there had been a thorough search made for hidden treasure. Piles of dried pelts lay scattered around, the richer prizes having evidently been carried off.

The raiders had doubtless shown rare discrimination as though among their number were those who themselves had once been trappers and therefore knew all about the value of black fox pelts, sables and mink that bring such top-notch prices in the fur markets of St. Louis and other busy places in the country.

Birdseye Baker led them through all this mess straight over to the door communicating with the factor's private room. This apartment also looked as if an earthquake of first dimensions had struck it and over on a cot against the further log wall they could see a man with a gray beard holding himself up on his elbow, having evidently heard strange voices and being filled with curiosity as well as wonder as to what all the fresh row was about.

"Hello there, Uncle Jimmy!" sang out Perk breezily as he pushed ahead with outstretched hand. "Ain't quite forgot Gabe Perkiser, have you, ol' top? Sorry to hear what's happened to you an' as me an' my boss, Mister John Jacob Astorbilt here, mean to head for the fort right away, we aim to get thet medicine man back to look after you. It happens we got a cloud chasin' airship waitin' outside to carry us wherever we wanter go."

The old Scotch factor looked as pleased as a man suffering from recent severe injuries might be expected to under the circumstances. He allowed the newcomer to squeeze his hand and even took Jack's who fancied the other from the first—the stern honesty of the man from bonny Scotland was to be seen in his clear eye and undismayed look.

"They treated me some scandalous, Perk," the injured man was saying with a quirk, but little in the way of Scotch brogue cropping up in his speech, "but ye ken I'm a tough old bird and have pulled out o' many a bad scrape in the past so it may be I'll weather this knockout, if only that doctor can gi'e me a fair start."

"Hamilton, they say his name is," ventured Perk, musingly, "somehow I don.t 'member the name, so like as not he must be a new one around here since I kicked out some years ago."

"Ay, that's the truth, laddie—he dropped in on us something like a year back, sayin' he was sick o' civilization and a' its cheats and wanted to live out his life where the primitive ways still held forth. I am o' the opinion the man must have met with some serious trouble — had his wife run awa' with a younger chap, more'n

likely, as they sometimes do, ye ken.   But for a'
that he's a clever physician and he'll pull me out
o' this slump if on'y he can be fetched before it's
too late."

CHAPTER XXII

PICKING UP CLUES

"Make your mind easy on that score, Uncle Jimmy," Perk went on to say as he bent over the wounded man, "we'll get up to the river post and my ol' haunts in a rush, pullin' out inside the hour an' either fetch the doctor back with us in the ship or on hossback, all that dependin' on how things happen to be with Colonel Ascot, who I understand is still in charge o' the Mounties."

Perk gave his mate a questioning glance as he said this, and was pleased to see Jack nod in the affirmative, as though thus putting the seal of his approval to the plan as given by his assistant.

"An' now, ol' friend," Perk continued in a soothing fashion, for he knew the Scotch nature of the other and could understand how the McGregor must be inwardly fuming concerning the robbery that had taken place and the losses to the great fur company of which he was an old and efficient official, "'fore we pull outen here you must let my boss take a look at them cuts an' bruises. It happens he's a fair surgeon—amatoor one, I mean—an' could fix you up to carry on till the reg'lar doc gets here. "How 'bout that, Jack?"

If either the factor or the ancient trapper noticed the rather odd familiarity existing between Perk and his supposedly wealthy employer, it did not strike them as strange—away up in this jumping-off place, as far as civilization was concerned, men were more or less equals, being judged more from what their accomplishments might be than from their money and besides, they doubtless remembered that Perk had always been a sort of free and easy independent fellow when with the Mounties.

"That's just about what we aim to do, Perk," Jack immediately told the other. "I don't claim to be much of a surgeon, but if there's anything I can do to stop the bleeding, or bind up the cuts, I'll be only too glad to lend a helping hand, Mr. McGregor."

He was as good as his word for inside of five minutes Jack had stripped off his coat, rolled up his shirt sleeves and commenced to examine the injuries suffered by the determined old factor when he dared take his life in his hands and try to defend the property of his employers.

It turned out that there were some pretty bad cuts and it was a wonder no fatal blows had been given for there could be little doubt that the aggressors shot and stabbed in a most reckless fashion. But evidently the factor's luck held good and Jack did not feel as though there was much danger of a fatal ending to the affair, providing no blood poisoning set in.

He called for warm water and clean cotton, which, being provided, he started to cleanse the wounds and apply some healing salve. So confidently did he work that the quaint looking old trapper, Birdseye, watching everything with wonder, might have been seen to nod his shaggy mane approvingly as though in his private opinion the young fellow was some surgeon indeed.

As he thus worked Jack entered into conversation with the factor, having two good reasons for doing so. He wished to distract the attention of his patient from himself and also to extract as much information as possible covering the recent raid. A description of the miscreants was given and especially of their savage leader known as the Hawk because of his faculty for striking a swift blow in one place and being heard of in another in such a short time as to make people believe he could fly like the speedy bird of prey.

"As far as I could say," Old Jimmy told him in answer to a question, "he's along about thirty years old, a shortish sort o' a man, quick as a flash in his movements and with eyes that bore

in like a gimlet might.   He's had his nose broken
at some time or other, which gives him a bit o'
a look like an eagle or a hawk.   It may be he got
his present name from that.   But he's a devil,
I'm thinking and ready to do anything, law or no
law when he smells rich booty in the game."

Jack gave Perk a knowing look accompanied
by a wink for that description, brief though it
might be, coincided with what had been in the
secret information sent by his chief at Washington—the broken nose stamped it as a positive
thing that the man he wanted was close at hand,
engaged in his same old line of business, that of
a hold-up man, robber of banks and payroll bandit with a record for masterly exploits second
to none.

So too with regard to the sudden surprise and
attack—it seemed as though the marauders must
have had accurate information as to when the
trading post would prove to be a rich prize and
also weakly defended.

"They had their plans a' set, I am fain to believe," the factor told him as though he had
somehow figured this out during the time he lay
there on his cot, "for ye ken it is only a few days
now when the customary Spring clean-up o' the
posts come to pass so they would know we had
rich pickings on hand. They lookit over the
whole o' the bales an' picked out a' the high-

priced pelts like they might be connoiseurs in that line, for I recognized twa former trappers in the gang—Squatty Bings an' Welchy, as tough an' hard drinkin' lads as ever lived."

"I've been told they left here just about three hours back — is that correct, Mr. McGregor?" asked Jack, wishing to make certain, for a great deal might depend on the question of elapsed time.

"I am no so sure, for I have not looked at my watch since being carried in the house," the factor informed him, "but Birdseye here would know, for he and the others were being herded in a bunch and kept under several guns. That was after I had been so badly mauled and lay helpless on the ground outside. They were in no great hurry—took their time, feasted on a' the food they could stow away—did a lot more up in bundles and wi' the choice pelts as well as a stock o' ammunition, finally pulled out, leaving the few men next to helpless since their guns had been carried awa'."

Taken in all, with a little imagination thrown in for good measure, Jack could picture the stirring happening as the outlaws, having accomplished all they planned to do, pulled up stakes and with jeering shouts as well as waving their hats defiantly, left the scene of their daring foray.

"They certainly had their inning," he observed as he finished his fairly decent surgical work and rose to his feet, "but I've an idea they're due for a little surprise before long when the tables may be turned. I came up here to hunt big game and if it happens to run on two legs, why, what's the odds? A lot depends on how the colonel of the Mounties happens to figure when he learns what's been going on around here—how these scoundrels are snapping their fingers and saying to the devil with the Mounties, whose glory has departed. I'm wondering just how it comes the Hawk and his crowd have been able to stave off arrest this long and if the reputation of your famous Northwest Police force has indeed been eclipsed."

"Don't you b'lieve that for a second, Jack!" cried the aroused Perk, jealous concerning the fame of the organization of which he used to be a proud member, "chances are they've been after this bunch right along an' even now may be settin' plans to net the hull gang—how 'bout that, Uncle Jimmy?"

"There have been a number of fierce fights within the past year between Colonel Ascot's troopers and the Hawk's gang—indeed, two of the Mounties have lost the number of their mess and three others had to be sent to the hospital at Winnipeg, seriously wounded in the encounters.

This Hawk is said to be the toughest nut ever doing business in all this great region. He seems to bear a charmed life and bullets fail to bring him down. The chances are, when you reach the post, it will be to find that some sort of expedition is off on a seemingly warm trail for whenever the Hawk plans to make one of his brilliant raids he always fixes things so that the troopers will at the same hour be many miles away, heading for some threatened post and out of communication."

Jack seemed very well satisfied with what he had gleaned — having been dispatched these many hundreds of miles just to apprehend this bandit, it pleased him to know what a thorn in the flesh Leonard Culpepper was proving to be in the lives of the guardians of the Northwest Territory.

Perk too, was grinning as if his thoughts might be rather pleasant.

"Huh! if that skunk could be picked up an' carried back to the States where he belongs," he went on to say with a chuckle, "I kinder guess Colonel Ascot he'd sleep some sounder. Wall, let's hope it'll come to pass afore many more days slip by."

Apparently neither Old Jimmy nor yet the ancient skin-gatherer Birdseye noticed how

Perk, a new-comer, seemed to know something they had never before heard, about the Hawk having drifted up from across the border but then in all the excitement taking place within the last few hours such a slip could pass unnoticed.

CHAPTER XXIII

THE NORTHWEST MOUNTED POLICE POST

It was now high time they were once more afloat.

Jack was well content to be on the wing since apparently nothing more was to be picked up at the devastated trading post. He and Perk should be heading for the station of the Mounties, so as to inform their commander with regard to what had happened at Frazer's, further south.

Accordingly, after telling the old factor not to worry as they meant to start the Mounties on the way to the scene of the outrage with the least possible delay, both he and Perk pressed the hand of the wounded man and passed outside, followed by the admiring Birdseye who would never cease from sounding the praises of Jack's surgical work.

The next thing to concern the pals was in line with their expected hop-off. Would it be possible to make the jump from such a wretched field, with its many bumpy spots calculated to cause the moving craft to wobble fiercely?

Together they walked over the anticipated course, examining the nature of the ground, to toss aside, when possible, such rocks as threatened to jar them seriously. When finally they had thus surveyed the entire stretch, Jack pronounced the decision in which his comrade concurred — that although they would assume some risks, still in the course of their experiences in the past both of them had successfully climbed out of even worse traps than the one they were now up against.

So they went aboard, watched by every living creature about the post saving Old Jimmy himself. As usual Jack checked his dials and the motor with a skill that only comes from long experience added to that peculiar air-minded wizardry possessed by just a few pilots, like Lindbergh.

"Okay Boss?" inquired Perk, picking up the ear-phones as if ready to adjust them to his head because it might be necessary for them to exchange remarks soon after they started, and according to Perk's mind it was very essential they should be prepared.

"Here we go!" came the answer, upon which the motor took hold and the big ship started forward, followed by the cheers of Birdseye and his fellows although these grew fainter as the amphibian went bumping along, increasing its pace as Jack saw fit to pull back the stick against his breast, until just as they finally lost contact with the ground, the racket of motor and propeller smothered all other sounds completely.

They were off to a safe start and no damage done. Perk settled down in his seat ready to take up his accustomed duties although he felt convinced everything was in apple-pie condition aboard the boat.

Their course was a point off due north, Perk having coached his mate with regard to that important matter. Besides, from their lofty lookout point it would soon be easy enough to discern the post known as Fort Laney for it lay on one of the small rivers that emptied into the Mackenzie, itself starting in Great Slave Lake.

Perk could not but remark upon the changes that were gradually taking place in the country the further north they went. This struck him as wonderful, for although he had spent several years in this region, never before had he been privileged to take such a sweeping survey of the landscape as on the present occasion for heretofore he had been upon the ground where rocky mountains and all manner of huge obstacles obstructed the view and restricted the vision.

He could figure out just about in what quarter

the Peace River lay, a place he had good occasion to remember since one of the most stirring adventures connected with his service in the Mounties had taken place on its banks. So too, was he able to look in the direction whence must lie the town of Simpson, on the great Mackenzie, some hundred miles or more distant as the crow flies. There was also Great Bear Lake, another body of water he had looked upon, and which must stir up other vivid memories for events in which he had taken a leading part, connected with the arrest of a notorious halfbreed, terrorizing the region roundabout, had brought him rather close to a fade-out since he met with serious wounds in the resulting scrimmage before he and his pal were able to overcome the desperado.

In this way Perk was indulging in recollections of past events that seemed very agreeable, to judge from the beaming smile he wore as he kept using the binoculars in order to pick out familiar scenes as they loomed upon his vision from time to time.

Then all at once Perk showed positive signs of excitement.

"Hi! there partner, let me take the controls for a spell! Want you to have the glasses and pick up that caribou jumpin' off away yonder jest on t'other side o' them birches that stand out so white'n clear."

Jack lost no time in doing as he was bidden for thus far it had never been his good fortune to glimpse a real caribou outside of a zoo and the thought of watching one on its native heath and feeding ground gave him quite a little thrill.

"Get him yet?" demanded Perk anxiously, seeing that Jack was moving the binoculars along as though their swift passage was carrying them past the patch of birch trees.

"Sure do, buddy," admitted the other, to add: "Looks like he might be close enough to eat out of my hand—keepin' an eye on this crate all right, as if he didn't just like our looks. There, he sprang off like an express train on the transcontinental railroad and I've lost him in the thick bush. I'd like to knock over one of his breed while we're up here but hardly think I'd be justified in staying around a single day longer than is absolutely necessary."

It turned out, however, Jack did get an opportunity to do that very thing, but of which event more anon.

He again took over the stick, being desirous of handling the ship when later on they reached the river post and started to drop down on the stream for a stop-over, long or short, neither of them knew just then.

Ten minutes later Perk made his announce-
ment.

"I c'n make out the barracks as plain as anything, with the river just beyond. We'll be there
in a jiffy, partner! How it all comes back to
me, the interestin' life I led up here with the
boys — I'll sure miss that Davis lad who, I
learned, was one o' the pair got killed in the fight
with that bloody-minded Hawk. Claude Davis
had an old mother livin' in Toronto, an' many
a time he used to tell me things 'bout his fambly
that made me think I knowed the hull passel o'
'em. Poor old lady, it must a near killed her when
she heard how her lad laid down his life for his
country. I always did claim these splended
Mounties up here, forever ready to take great
risks to protect the scattered settlers, are soldiers
jest as much as those o' us who served in the big
scrap across the Atlantic. But look ahead, Jack,
an' you c'n see the post now with the naked eye.
Yeah, and as sure as you live there's a Mounty
steppin' up from the boats, carryin' what looks to
me like a string o' fish! Gee whiz! how many
times did I furnish the fish course for lots o' dinner messes. Seems like 'twas on'y yesterday, or
the day 'fore, since I put my teeth in a cold-
water fish from that river which empties into the
Polar Sea."

Presently they were circling the post, running

out over the river which Jack was eyeing closely, as if to make certain it offered plenty of excellent opportunities toward making a landing. At least he had been assured there was sufficient water at almost any point to answer their purpose, the stream being high at this particular season of the year when so much snow had been melting all through the watershed which the river drained.

"See," cried the alert Perk, "sev'ral more o' the crowd have rushed out o' the barracks, knowin' from the shouts that chap set up somethin' out o' the ordinary was on the bills. But jest the same I kinder guess a bunch o' the boys must be away right now. What did we hear 'bout that cunnin' snake, the Hawk gen'rally outsmartin' the Mounties by makin' a sham attack on some place so's to send a posse whoopin' thataways while he proceeded to play his own game unmolested fifty miles away, an' never a uniform in sight?"

"Going down—lower floor—hold your breath, Perk!" cried the pilot as he shut off the engine and, thrusting the nose of his craft sharply downward, proceeded to start a swift dive toward the river a thousand feet below.

Perk could not restrain his enthusiasm, but standing half erect waved his hat excitedly, also letting loose a few frightfully loud yells that must have been eye-openers to the several uniformed Mounties standing close to the river's edge, watching in sheer amazement the swoop of the descending aerial cabin plane.

CHAPTER XXIV

READY TO START

'A splash, a short run upstream and the amphibian was riding the little waves like a duck. Then as Jack once more turned on his power they taxied in close to the bank where a wing would serve as a gang-plank to get them ashore.

"Hello! ol' hoss Red Lowden!" bawled Perk, in a glow of excitement.

One of the Mounties, with the marks of a sergeant on his sleeve, exhibited great excitement at hearing himself thus addressed so familiarly by a party who, up to that moment, he had not recognized owing chiefly to the aviator's goggles and helmet, which were now hastily removed as Perk jumped ashore.

"Gabe Perkiser!" the sergeant gasped, apparently staggered at learning the identity of one of the flyers.

They met and shook hands with enthusiasm, for in those days of old they had been boon companions.

Perk put a finger on his lips.

"Go slow 'bout callin' me by that name, brother," he told the other, half under his breath. "Jest now I'm sailin' under false colors, as you might say. I'm in Uncle Sam's Secret Service, an' known as Gabe Smith, a Maine woods guide in the employ o' a rich gent, a real sport an' big game hunter—let me introduce him to you Red —Mister John Jacob Astorbilt," and with the last word he gave the wearer of the uniform a wicked wink that spoke volumes to Red, who nodded and shook hands with Jack.

He could give a pretty clever guess as to who and what this determined looking young fellow must be and the story could keep until a more convenient season.

"Glad to meet you, Mr. Astorbilt," he went on to say aloud for the benefit of the two other Mounties hovering close by with the design of being made acquainted with the newcomers.

They were both wise and seasoned members of the force, although Perk was meeting them for the first time and thus judged they had been transferred from another post during his absence.

"I hope Colonel Ascot is well," remarked Jack softly as he stood there close beside Red Lowden, "I am anxious to meet him, for I have a strong suspicion he will be deeply interested in certain documents I am bearing with me, both from Ottawa in your Dominion here and also from my Big Boss at Washington, D. C."

The other, who was a sturdy specimen of Canadian manhood, with the eye of a hawk, nodded his head and looked wise as he hastened to say:

"Wait till I introduce you to these members of our patrol and then I'll lead you to the Colonel, who is doing a bit of official correspondence inside his office close by."

This was soon accomplished and as the sportsman in search of fresh thrills Jack met the couple of Mounties. Leaving Perk chatting with them he followed the sergeant into the long, low log barracks where in a cubbyhole at the end they found a tall, severe looking man, dressed in the garb of an officer, seated at a desk and busily engaged in writing.

He must have heard all the commotion outside connected with the arrival of the cloud-chaser, but being deeply interested in what he was writing and too much given to decorum to display any vulgar curiosity, he had remained there.

But after all he turned out to be very much a gentleman as well as a fine disciplinarian, as Jack speedily learned for after he had explained just who he was and what the nature of his long flight into the wilderness contemplated, he found

Colonel Ascot vastly interested and sympathetic.

Red Lowden had discreetly withdrawn, saluting as he went so Jack and the commandant of the frontier post were alone in the office.

"I wish to assure you, young man," observed the Colonel again cordially sqeezing Jack's hand, "you are bringing me the finest possible news. This knave has been playing the very devil around the whole sector and so far has had us guessing. The hardest nut we've had to crack in the entire term of my service in the corps. If by any great luck we can combine our forces and accomplish his capture, I shall feel myself in your debt beyond measure.

Jack was gratified at hearing these frank and hearty words.

"I have a companion with me, Colonel," he further observed, "a reliable chap in the bargain and a clever aviator. He once had the honor to serve under you up here—Gabe Perkiser.

He saw a pleased expression flit across the grim face of the commandant and judged that Perk must have been something of a favorite with the Colonel.

"Glad to hear that, sir," the latter told his visitor, nodding his head in approval. "Perk was a credit to the uniform all the time he was with us in our job of rounding up disturbers of the peace and guarding honest men against such rascals and blackguards as continually drift up to this country. They seem to think its loneliness will guarantee them immunity from the long arm of the law they have flaunted. I'll be pleased to see him again—and in the service you represent so creditably, as I can well imagine."

"We look for a bit of assistance from your force, Colonel," continued Jack, "and you will find your authority for giving us a helping hand in these documents from your head office," with which he handed the other a small packet of official looking papers.

"I can take everything you say for granted, Mr.—er Astorbilt but am sorry you have dropped in on us at a most unfortunate time, since the majority of my men are away—there came a sudden call for assistance at a little settlement of newcomers some fifty miles distant— it was believed a raid was contemplated by this desperado, the Hawk. The letter was signed by a man whom I happened to know stood in the light of a leader in that community, and although I may have had my secret misgivings I felt compelled to start a squad off late last evening. They will hardly get back here under the best of conditions for another forty-eight hours; and even at that their mounts will be far from fresh for another wild dash."

Jack had even figured on something like this

coming to pass, and in his mind laid out a plan of campaign.

"We have come direct from the Frazer trading-post, Colonel," he hastened to explain; "it was taken by trickery last night, the old factor seriously wounded, and the post robbed of everything of value, including precious pelts, food, ammunition, and all else."

Colonel Ascot looked greatly annoyed.

"Then my fears were justified," he went on to say, with a grimace, and a shrug of his shoulders; "never has that man's equal been known in all the years I've been up against clever crooks. It was a false appeal for help, intended to employ most of my men, and give these desperate looters plenty of time to get away with their plunder. Under the unfortunate circumstances what can I do to further your plans, sir? Anything in my power you may command—I have but three of my force at the post, being short-handed just at present, as several are on leave of absence for special reasons."

"If you could spare me Sergeant Lowden, sir, whom my comrade has recommended highly as one with a thorough knowledge of the whole country for fifty miles around, and allow me to carry the doctor back to Frazer's to take charge of poor Old Jimmy, I could, I believe, make good progress; especially if you sent the balance of your detachment after us as an emergency force, in case we find the sledding a bit too rough."

Colonel Ascot looked relieved, as though a heavy load had been taken from his chest.

"Only too gladly will I accede to that request," he told his guest. "I am expecting Dr. Hamilton at any moment now, when you can meet him, and ask him to ride back with you to the trading post. He is a gentleman, and a very gifted surgeon—in the year and more that he's been in this neighborhood I have known him to perform almost unbelievable operations with the most remarkable success. There is some mystery about the man, which is none of our business — I am simply telling you in order that you may not unintentially permit yourself — or Perk, whose failings along the line of curiosity I know full well—to display any sign of butting in. In these lonely regions, my dear sir, just as in the gold fields, a man's past is his business only, and other people are content that it should remain a dead secret; but you can rest assured he is straight goods, and moreover a polished gentleman, as well as a wonderful physician."

"I can readily understand what you mean, Colonel," Jack warmly assured him, "and once I have warned Perk neither of us ever display the slightest curiosity about his hidden past—as you

say, it concerns him alone; we'll just take him
for what he is, and be glad to know him."

They talked further, as the Colonel glanced at
his papers and laid them in a pigeonhole of his
desk; and Jack learned a number of important
things connected with the man whom he planned
to take back with him to the States, having the
necessary documents to allow of this being done
via the airship route.

Then the officer asked him to step outside, for
he believed he had heard the voice of Dr. Hamilton, who it appeared, was coming once a day to
treat a badly lacerated leg of one of the privates,
who had been thrown from his horse amidst a
cache of unusually jagged rocks, with ill results.

Jack liked the doctor from the start, although
he could plainly see that something like grief —
hardly remorse—must have been eating at the
other's heart for many a moon, his manner was
so suppressed, so sad.

Of course the doctor hastened to assure him he
would be only too glad to take the long gallop to
the trading post, and do what was necessary for
Old Jimmy, whom he knew very well, and
esteemed highly.

"I am not much of a horseman, I'm afraid,"
he told Jack, whom he knew simply as a well-
to-do young gentleman, with a great love for out-
doors sports, and big game hunting chief of all;

"but the Colonel has an animal I've used before, and doubtless Romeo will carry me safely to the post, since the trail is fairly easy; but the distance is more than he could negotiate at one try, I'm thinking."

"That can be easily arranged," Jack explained; "we might be able to get halfway to our destination by the time darkness sets in, when we could make camp, spend the night beside the trail, and get an early morning start. And thank you very much, Doctor, for your kindness in going, I did all I could for a temporary dressing; but it was only the work of an amateur, and Jimmy really needs further attention."

"Which I shall be only too pleased to give, since I have the utmost regard for the old factor," which remark satisfied Jack that everything was coming along nicely.

CHAPTER XXV

AN OVERNIGHT BIVOUAC

Immediately the station took on an air of great commotion. Sergeant Red Lowden had been given secret instructions to accompany the two air voyagers, and was to go heavily armed, as for a battle. He was also told to place his services entirely at the disposal of the young fellow, as to whose real identity he had been "put wise" by Perk, while Jack and the commander had their little chat.

The horses were brought out from the log stable, supplies gathered and packed, and everything done that was needful when a force was starting off for "business at the old stand."

Of course Perk had met Dr. Hamilton, and been introduced under his fictitious cognomen of "Smith." He seemed a bit awed in the presence of the other, and kept watching him out of the tail of his eye—indeed, from that time on Perk showed signs of being deeply interested in the strange man, for he would steal a glance in his direction, shake his head as if "all balled up," to quote his own words as spoken later on; and then go into one of his rare silent spells as if cudgeling those slow moving wits of his.

Jack had of course taken occasion to tell Perk what the Colonel had passed along concerning the doctor; and being duly impressed with the need of caution had solemnly promised never to evince the slightest curiosity in connection with the unknown past history.

"Queer, how I seem to keep thinkin' I've met up with him somewhere or other," he managed at one time to mention to his chum, just before they got word from Red Lowden that everything was ready for the start; "but shucks! that same could hardly be possible, since he on'y bobbed up hereabouts sixteen moons back, Red tells me; and I'd been out o' this country a few moons 'fore that. Kinder guess I must be pokin' in the wrong prairie-dog hole, an' it's jest a case o' mistaken identity, as some calls it when you're follerin' the false trail. Let it go at that, partner; an' here comes Red to tell us we gotter to jump-off."

Jack had made all arrangements for his ship to be taken care of during his absence; whether it was for three days, a week, or even much longer the commandant assured him nothing should happen to endanger the amphibian; which would lie there tied up alongside the river bank, with some one keeping a jealous eye on the same day and night.

So they shook hands with Colonel Ascot, who wished them all success in the undertaking they had planned out.

"Please God you may live to come back here later on, my friends," he said, with a warmth Perk had never seen him exhibit before; "and that success will attend you in this undertaking. Depend upon it the posse will follow after you as soon as it is practicable; and Red there will show you how we leave a clue along the road as we go, for those coming in the rear to follow — that will be after you quit Frazer's, and start in on the real tough part of the trip."

Which assurance afforded Jack more or less satisfaction, for he somehow had an idea they might find the bunch of desperadoes a bit too tough to be successfully handled by such a small force; and be compelled to fall back until joined by the re-inforcements.

They mounted, and were off at a gallop, sometimes in single file, and again doubling up when the trail widened in places.

Red took the advance, since he was so thoroughly acquainted with every rod of the trail that led to the fur-trading post. Then followed Jack, with Perk at his heels, and the doctor bringing up the rear.

Whenever they struck a section where the trail broadened out Perk never lost an opportunity to ride alongside his chum; and of course always had a few of his interminable questions to ask; just as though to him Jack represented an encyclopedia that could supply all his numerous wants, if only properly "tapped"—Perk being from Maine, must have many times made maple sugar in the bush; and tapping trees for the sap evidently had brought him to ply the same methods when in need of information.

Perk had of course taken his faithful hand machine gun, being under the impression that it would come in handy when the time for action arrived. So, too, had Jack fastened his fine repeating sporting rifle to his saddle—it was just such a handsome weapon as he had always longed to own for hunting purposes, and hence he took advantage of his assumed personality to make the purchase — especially since generous Uncle Sam would stand back of the extravagance, since one could hardly expect to pose successfully in the guise of an ambitious big game hunter unless he possessed such a necessary Winchester.

After all the packages containing "grub" had been affixed to the saddles of the party, Perk had come climbing out of the cabin of the ship carrying what appeared to be a mysterious black leather hand-grip—just what it contained he did not attempt to explain even to his old-time pal Red. As Jack however glimpsed the strange object he seemed to smile comprehendingly, as if he might commend his comrade for going prepared for great emergencies — of this matter more may be said later on, when events begin to thicken, and the air becomes saturated with exciting happenings.

Although making good time Red was too old a campaigner to force things, especially at such an early stage of the journey. To be sure they stood to reach Frazer's some hours after daylight at the earliest, and the raiders would have a long start of them; but as Red had confided to Jack, he was in possession of more recent knowledge covering the suspected secret lair of the looters; and besides, was he not the acknowledged peer of any Indian or halfbreed in all the Northwest country when it came to following a trail?

Jack was well satisfied with his chances for running the wily Hawk to his hidden den; what came to pass after that had been accomplished must depend on how cleverly they could carry on, so as to catch the enemy napping, and pounce upon him unawares. While believing fully in his maxim of being prepared, Jack was not the one to give himself useless worry, leaving all that for the time when he must bring his reserve powers into play.

The afternoon fell away, with the sun dropping lower down the western sky. In less than another hour they would find twilight encompassing them, and must therefore pick out some likely camping spot, where fresh water would be handy, and plenty of desirable fuel nearby to keep their fire during the coming night.

Later on Red began to keep his eye "peeled" for a site that possessed, in addition to rising ground, all these other requirements. He did not mean to let such a spot pass him by, even though the hour was still early, lest another could not be reached, and they must find themselves deprived of certain comforts—Red, you see, was a bit like Perk in that respect—he had great respect for his stomach, and would make considerable other sacrifices in order that a proper cooking fire could be utilized, and a sufficiency of food prepared to fill the expected vacuum.

Just a short time before the glowing ball of fire in the west sank behind the upward thrust of the mountain peaks, Red gave a cry, and held up his hand as a signal that the afternoon gallop was at an end.

A tempting little brooklet ran gurgling along

its way alongside the trail, and a finer campsite it would have been hard to find. The timber was fairly thick, with a small open glade close by. The trees gave considerable protection for travelers without a tent, or other shelter; but then Red and Perk knew how to throw up a rude shack from material that was conveniently handy, in case rain threatened, which was not likely just then, these pioneers of the wide spaces agreed on this special occasion.

Dr. Hamilton for one was glad the ride had come to an end; he did not pretend to be much of a horseman, and the constant contact with a hard saddle proved anything but pleasant or agreeable to him, though never a single word of complaint had escaped his lips.

Perk set about helping Red gather a pile of wood, after quenching his thirst at the brook, the water being as cool as they could wish. They had been wise enough to fetch blankets for the crowd, and with a fire going all night long, no one could reasonably complain.

Jack and the doctor sat there chatting on subjects that seemed to engage them both, while watching with interest as the two others started getting supper. Taken altogether it was quite a cheery picture, as Jack could not help remarking; to find that his companion quite agreed with him; from which Jack decided that after all the physician could not be naturally diffident to the charm of camping out, although admitting that he was hardly more than a novice along those lines.

Perk certainly acted as if vastly pleased with the opportunity to get up another open air meal —how he did detest those periods of partaking of what he sneeringly called "flying fare" such as became necessary so often while he and Jack were on the wing, and putting the miles behind them when on business bent—if he had his way about things they would have landed at each and every day's end, and had their meals like civilized human beings instead of "sky hoboes."

It was really a tempting supper that the pair of outdoor men managed to serve. They ranged along a convenient log, rolled into position by the culinary artists, always with an eye out for comfort; and here Jack and Dr. Hamilton were given heaping pannikins of solid food, that tasted "pretty fine"; nor was the accompanying coffee anything to be scorned, for Perk certainly knew just how to brew it to bring out all its hidden aroma, and tempt every one to come back for a second cup.

They sat there before a blazing fire and talked of many things; yet studiously avoiding any and all reference to the one subject uppermost in the minds of at least three of the number—the chances of success they might meet in endeavoring to track the reckless lawbreaker, known as the Hawk, to his lair, and either taking him prisoner, or, if forced to extreme measures, effectually winding up his audacious exploits by putting him under the sod.

Jack soon realized that his first estimation of Dr. Hamilton was absolutely correct; for the other entered into the conversation as though pleased to meet up with one who was so well up in matters of the day as Jack proved to be.

They were all more or less fatigued by the hard three hours' gallop along the twisting trail, over mountain slopes, and through valleys that lay between; so it was not long before first the doctor made up his blanket bed and crawled within; then Jack a little later followed suit; and finally, after fixing the campfire so it would continue to burn for some hours, Perk and Red also "kicked off," as the former expressed it. After that silence deep and profound fell upon the scene, where nearby the horses securely hobbled cropped spears of grass such as they could reach; and in the end also settled down for a complete rest.

CHAPTER XXVI

THE WOLF PACK

Jack, chancing to awaken several hours afterwards sat up to rearrange his blanket. The fire was burning fairly well, so that he could easily see objects within a certain range.

A slight movement drew his attention toward the spot where Dr. Hamilton had rolled himself up in the blanket assigned to his use; and Jack could see him sitting there, with his head bowed down as though, unable to sleep, he was indulging in sombre thoughts.

Somehow Jack had been drawn toward the strange man, whom he felt confident must have some deep reason for coming to this outpost of civilization, and burying both himself and his rare talents under an assumed identity.

"He's certainly got something gnawing at his heart, by the way he acts," Jack told himself, as he snuggled down again within the folds of his covers. "And somehow I just can't seem to believe he's a bad man—his face, so sad, and yet sympathetic, belies that. Still, the secret is his own, and none of my business."

So he put it out of his mind, and was soon fast asleep once more. When next he awoke it must have been several hours later, as he could tell by glancing up at the star-studded heavens; for Jack had studied the planetary system, and could tell how the night was passing fairly well by the time of the setting of the various celestial orbs.

The fire was burning brightly, showing that either Perk or Red must have been keeping tabs on its care, having recently replenished the fuel supply.

"Pretty soft, I'd call it," chuckled Jack, again dropping back to catch a "few more winks" of sleep before the coming of dawn; "but say, what's the use of having a chum who calls himself an old woods guide along, to look after you, if he doesn't give you all the service he's supposed to supply for his wages? We'll have many a good laugh over this delightful arrangement in other days and nights."

Three of the horses were lying down, the fourth trying to find a few more stray wisps of green stuff by reaching out to the extent of his tethering rope. All seemed well with the world, and Jack judged it the part of wisdom to fight off dull cares until the time really arrived for action.

Then for the third time he opened his eyes and

began to stretch his limbs, by that time feeling a bit cramped from his lying in a certain position so long.

"Must be getting daylight," he told himself, noting how he could see objects at some little distance beyond the smouldering campfire; but as it was not the proper caper for a supposed young millionaire sportsman to be the first on stirring in camp, Jack concluded to just lie there and do a little calculating, having in mind the stirring drama they were likely to run into ere another day had come to an end.

"Huh! now, what in thunder does all that distant racket mean?"

Of course that was Perk muttering to himself, and turning his head Jack could see the other rising to a sitting position, with his head set on one side, as though he were straining his hearing.

This caused Jack to suddenly realize for the first time that it was not only the gurgling of the nearby running brook he had been hearing—somewhere within half a mile other sounds were rising, and even gradually drawing closer right along—yapping, for all the world like dogs chasing a rabbit, or a sly fox caught out with dawn coloring the sky.

Jack hastened to sit up.

"Yes, what can it be, do you think, Perk?" he asked, quietly.

"Awake are you, ol' hoss?" the other went on to say though without turning his head. "Sounds like wolves, or I'd say kiotes only I happen to know they ain't any sech animals 'way up here—leastways I never did run across sech all the time I rode 'round this section o' country."

"A pack of timber wolves, you mean, buddy—the big, gray chaps that can pull down a deer as easy as a mountain lion would do the job?"

"Them's the kind like enough, Jack," affirmed the other.

"The chase is on then, it seems, Perk; what d'ye reckon they're after?"

"Some sorter game they're meanin' to make a breakfast off'n—mebbe a cow moose, or else it might be a caribou, partner," Perk went on to say, as if mildly interested. "Huh! wouldn't mind havin' a juicy caribou steak myself for breakfast, on'y it'd be breakin' the game laws to shoot sech a critter out o' season. Say, they must be headin' this way, Jack, ol' pard!"

"Either that, or else there's a change of wind," agreed the other; "for the racket grows louder right along."

Perk reached out and laid his hand on the ever faithful machine-gun, which it seemed he had carefully placed alongside on settling **down** for the night.

"I guess now I'll get up, an' toddle out by that openin' in the timber," Jack heard him saying; "mebbe we might have the good luck to look-in on the gay scrap, if the beggars bring their quarry to bay close by here. Anyhow it's plumb mornin', an' plenty to do."

Jack could not have told had he been asked why he should copy Perk's example, possessing himself of the Winchester repeater, and even following his comrade in the direction of the open glade, toward which the suggestive sounds appeared to be heading.

There, too, was Red Lowden starting to "climb out" of his swathing blanket, apparently recognizing the fact that there might be something interesting on the carpet worth witnessing. All this movement must have aroused the doctor, for Jack noticed a movement in his quarter, as though the exodus from the camp were about to be made unanimous.

Jack and Perk dropped down on the edge of the opening.

"That's in our favor," the latter was whispering—"the wind, what little there happens to be ablowin' is comin' right in our face, so the pesky beasts ain't agoin' to scent us right away. I kinder guess they's so crazy worked up over git-in' a breakfast they ain't so cunnin' as usual. Wow! they're sure closin' in on the dick, that's flat—I c'n notice a change in the yelpin' that tells the story. Steady now, ol' hoss, for here they come aswoopin'!"

Jack crouched low, with staring eyes—there was something that bordered on the thrilling about this dramatic panorama of the wilderness which a freak of good fortune was bringing under their observation—he even felt his heart beating as fast as a throbbing rivetting machine, such as he remembered once hearing at work on a skyscraper in the building in New York City— in fact, Jack rather fancied this was as close an approach to the real "buck ague" as he had ever experienced, for while "some hunter" he did not claim to be a veteran in the chase.

Suddenly some large object broke out from the scrub on the other side of the open glade—it was a bull caribou, all right, and extremely winded, the chase having evidently been a long and thrill- ing one. Gone was much of the spring to its gait, usually as swift as the wind—the pertinacity of its four-footed pursuers had completely worn the caribou out, and all that was left was for him to turn on the pack, and battle until they dragged him down by the weight of numbers, backed by ferocious hunger.

There in the centre the gallant old fellow

whirled around and stood at bay, just as Jack had seen in a celebrated engraving. One sweep of his half-developed antlers and a daring wolf was flung ruthlessly aside, to come back limping, but as eager as ever.

It was a spectacle Jack would not have missed for anything; and yet all his sympathies were for the poor stag, so sorely beset by those ravenous foes. Again and again did he strike out and scatter his enemies; but his condition this early in the season was not as hardened as would have been the case along toward late in the Fall months, so that his blows failed to cripple those he sent flying right and left.

Perk was on one knee, and with his machine-gun lifted halfway to his shoulder, as though the inclination to mix in the scrimmage had begun to grip him too powerfully to be long resisted.

The crisis came with lightning-like rapidity, and it turned out just about as Jack had anticipated would be the case. One of the half-dozen wolves made a bold leap just when the caribou, having sent another flying, was caught off his guard. He landed on the stag's quarter, and fastened his teeth in his flank. That served to disconcert the doomed animal, so that a second of his persecutors was enabled to fasten on his neck, and weight him down.

That hastened the inevitable end to the woods

tragedy. There was no longer heard the yelps of the triumphant wolves—only a terrible snapping sound, and a mad scrambling, as the gallant caribou stag kept up the unequal fight, evidently determined to resist "to the last ditch."

Perk had reached the end of his rope; he could no longer resist the temptation to throw his glove into the arena, and take up the cause of the weaker one of the contenders

Jack heard the sudden crash of the machine-gun close to his ear. One of the maddened wolves fell at the report, to get up no more. A second bit the dust almost immediately afterwards, for Perk had only to swing his gun in a small section of a half-circle to spray the carnivora in succession.

Panic gripped those still remaining—possibly for the first time they whiffed the scent of human foes; so, too, they may have known what that crash of firearms, those spitting flashes of flame signified.

Waiting not upon the order of their going they abandoned all hopes of a well earned meal, and made off like so many streaks.

Perk ceased firing—he also gave a little whoop, as if triumph filled his veins with exaltation that must find some sort of vent.

"Hot ziggetty dig! jest see the cowardly critter lope out o' here, will you, partner?" was the burden of his shout, as the remainder of the lupine pack disappeared among the tree-trunks well beyond; "but what a danged shame the poor caribou's so bad hurt he jest can't move off—there, by the great horn spoon if he ain't laid down on the job; I kinder guess I hit in a little bit too late to help him any."

As they approached the wretched victim of wolfish hunger and ferocity attempted to get on his legs again; but seemed too weak to do more than lift himself halfway, when he once more fell back.

"Better we put him out of his misery, Perk," Jack suggested, knowing full well that the animal was doomed, no matter what they did; for if left to himself the wolf pack—what was left of it at any rate—was bound to return, and finish their slaughter.

"You do it, brother," begged Perk, "somehow I don't seem able to jest up an' knock him on the head. Your rifle's a heap better for that job."

"It will be a mercy, since he's done for, no matter how we look at it," the other went on to say; "so, game law or not, I've just got to do it."

With the speedy crack of his thirty-thirty sporting rifle the caribou gave one expiring kick, and then lay there limp and lifeless.

Jack surveyed his victim, and shook his head

as though he took no pleasure whatever in the act of mercy.

"Since necessity forced us into this game, Perk, there's no reason why you shouldn't have your caribou steak for breakfast; though I've got an idea it may give your grinders some job, from toughness. Go to it, brother; if you pronounce it eatable I may try a small portion myself, though I'm not building up any high hopes as to enjoying it."

Since it was daylight, and they were all aroused, they concluded there was no sense of "making two bites of a cherry." Accordingly Perk coaxed Red to build up a good cooking-fire, while he proceeded to cut some slices from the intact flank of the fallen stag.

At any rate it had an appetizing flavor while cooking, that caused Red to look expectant. Jack took a small portion on his pannikin, and started to masticate it in sections; but just the same he failed to clear off his plate, which would indicate that he hardly approved of that kind of venison.

From the fact that Perk did not see fit to select any more of the meat to carry along when they pulled out, one of three things must have affected him—either he did not anticipate having another chance to make use of a cooking fire in the near future; felt a bit worried as to what would happen if a game-warden, roving far afield, should happen along while he put in time at his culinary labors; or else even he had found the venison too tough for mastication—possibly a bit of all three reasons influenced him in abandoning the remainder of the carcass to those hungry brutes, undoubtedly still hovering in ambush not far away.

Then Jack called out "boots and saddles," with the whole four mounting their waiting steeds, and galloping along the trail.

CHAPTER XXVII

ON THE DANGEROUS TRAIL

The horses being fresh after the all-night bivouac, the little party made good time along the crooked trail. Perk was enjoying himself to the limit, taking in all the old familiar sights— how well he remembered different happenings that were connected with this, or that special spot; indeed, he found it hard to believe some years had passed since he followed this path between Frazer's trading-post of the great Hudson's Bay Fur Company, and the Mounties' further north station.

It was going on nine when they again came in sight of the long log building that housed the factor and his belongings—such as Hawk and his bold crowd had left untouched during their recent raid.

All seemed peaceful at the post, although the ashes marking the burned annex told how some unusual event must have recently taken place.

They found Old Jimmy getting along as well as could be expected, but anxious for the coming of the doctor, in whom he had every confidence in the world. A superficial examination quickly put Dr. Hamilton in possession of sufficient knowledge upon which to base a verdict.

"Nothing very serious, McGregor," he told the factor, in a cheery tone that did much to dissipate any fears the other may have entertained as to the outcome of his wounds.

Jack and Perk too, were relieved, for both of them had reason to feel a burden was lifted from their hearts—Perk because of his old friendship for the factor; and Jack on account of his having given "first aid" to the victim of the lawless Hawk's latest raid.

Turning to Jack Dr. Hamilton surveyed him with kindling eyes.

"If, as you said, young man," he told the flyer, "you are only an amateur at handling cases like this, I want to tell you everything has been carried out in a way that would not have shamed the best of surgeons. Jimmy will owe a lot to your skillful work. And let me further say most earnestly, that if at some future date it ever occurs to you to change your profession, should you choose to follow that of surgery, I can easily predict a more than ordinary success awaits you— remember that, Jack."

"Can you tie that?" burst out the grinning Perk, who seemed more tickled at hearing these words of praise than was the blushing recipient himself. "I kinder guessed my best pal was top-notch 'long them lines when I watched him ado-in' his stuff. So Jack, in case you ever do get knocked out o' the cloud-chasin' game, plenty o' time left to climb up the ladder in the surgical ward."

Jack hurriedly left the room, although it would have been only natural for him to feel a little thrill at being thus praised by a professional man whom he had already begun to hold in high esteem.

Perk joined him outside, but was kept from doing much talking by the necessity of carrying out a number of needful errands. They did not expect to waste any unnecessary time hanging about the post—the trail was already cold, and it was essential that they get on the move as speed-ily as possible. Jack well knew what difficult, and perhaps even sanguine work still remained to be accomplished, and as usual was eager to get it all over with.

"We can't hang fire in this business," he was telling Perk, who perhaps did not look at things in quite the same light, since his nature differed from that of his companion; "and until I see our man trussed up, to await our pleasure in hop-ping off for the border, I'll not have a peaceful moment. From now on this has to be a whirlwind campaign, and no mistake—get that, partner?"

"Huh! pleases me okay, ol' hoss," the other told him, nodding his head vigorously; "I'm in the game up to my neck, an' with me it sure is 'Pike's Peak—or Bust!'"

"We'll take a little time to look over our stuff," suggested Jack, the always wise worker, who seldom left the slightest thing undone, and consequently, like other cautious sky pilots, seldom had a real accident overtake him. "Make sure you've got plenty of cartridges for your gun, and than add another belt for good measure, because you never can tell what may happen, and it's best to be on the safe side—as a fire insurance agent once said on his advertising cards, it's 'better to *have* insurance, and not *need* it; than to *need* insurance and not *have* it.'"

"Yeah! I know it, Jack, boy," admitted Perk, "even if sometimes I do get caught nappin', an' have a peck o' trouble 'count o' my carelessness. I'm set to carry along every shell I fetched up here with me—this is the job they're meant for, an' why be a miser 'bout it?"

"That's the ticket, partner," Jack told him, apparently quite satisfied he had started his companion on the right road—Perk sometimes had to be "shown," and then he would follow to the bitter end.

Red Lowden had also been making sure noth
ing was forgotten, so far as he could tell. Of
course he was somewhat in the dark as to just
what means Jack meant to employ in order to
bring about the success of the undertaking; but
in the short time he had known the young Secret
Service detective he had realized the capacity
the other exhibited for handling just such intri
cate cases—if it were not so the astute Head of
the Organization at Washington would never
have entrusted this difficult problem to his hands.

Of course, from this time forward it would be
Sergeant Lowden who would take the lead, since
he knew the country, and it was all a puzzle to
Jack—even Perk would not be half as well
acquainted with the ground as the one who for
a dozen years had been going over the entire district for a radius of probably fifty miles in all
directions.

Then, too, should any difficulty arise they
could put their heads together, and find a solu-
tion to the problem, since many hands make light
work, according to the old saying.

While Jack and Perk were doing other things
Red had taken a look at the tracks left by the
raiders. Luckily no rain had fallen since they
galloped away from the plucked post, and hence
the imprints of their animals' hoofs could still be
plainly located.

Besides this, Red was depending considerably on certain secret information lately drifting in to Colonel Ascot, to help him out—as yet he had not said anything to Jack and Perk concerning this matter, but anticipated taking them both into his confidence before long, as it was essential they should understand just what resources he was banking upon in order to run the wolves to their secret den, the whereabouts of which had so long been unknown.

And so, about an hour after arriving at Frazer's, the trio again rode forth, to bring about the finishing touches of their campaign.

Even Perk seemed sobered by the desperate character of the duties now devolving on the little party. Outnumbered at least two to one, possibly with even greater odds against them, they would surely need all the boldness and strategy with which they were endowed, in order to bring about a successful finish to the invasion of the enemy's stronghold.

Sometimes they were compelled to go single-file on account of the narrow trail, alongside which great masses of mighty rocks were piled up; but in other places it was possible to ride three abreast; and these were the occasions when Jack and Red consulted, clearing up any foggy spots, so that they could work in unison when the time came for action.

Not a single incident occurred to take their attention from the fact that they were carrying their lives in their hands.   Now and then the guide would pull up in order that he might make use of the binoculars (which Jack had taken pains to bring along) some suspicious clump of rocks such as would afford a most effective spot for an ambush needed closer observation; and Red was too cautious a ranger to rush into a trap when it could be avoided.

As they progressed Jack noticed how their guide gradually slowed down; from which cirsumstance he judged they must be nearing the hidden retreat of the plunderers.   It gave him increased confidence in the sagacity of the Mounty sergeant, whose disposition corresponded more or less with his own.

Coming to a delightfully cold spring that bubbled up close to the trail, Red called a halt.

"A short rest will breathe the hosses," Red was saying, after he had taken a good look at the trail beyond the wayside spring; "and by the same token I think it's high time I told you both about a little trick of luck that came my way just a week or so back; 'specially since it's got so much to do with the carrying out of this surround, and hoped-for haul."

CHAPTER XXVIII

DODGING THE LOOKOUT

Perk looked eagerly at his old pal when Sergeant Red made that interesting disclosure. The three of them were sitting close to the spring at the time, engaged in passing a collapsible metal cup from hand to hand, and quenching their thirst from the clear water that came forth in apparently inexhaustible quantities.

"Huh! I kinder guessed now, Red, ol' hoss, that you had a trump cyard up your sleeve all this while—reckon I ain't forgot a trick you used to play on us boys long ago, springin' a nice little surprise just when the game looked the bunk, an' we reckoned we was up a stump. Hit it up then, an' tell us what sorter good luck it was you run smack up against, that's got somethin' to do with this here racket o' ourn."

"I was riding slowly back to the station, after taking our mail to the nearest settlement, where it could go on its way by a carrier, when I chanced to hear what sounded like a groan. Of course I first of all suspected it might be some sort of slick trap to get me off my mount; but

230

after riding on a bit I dismounted and fastening my hoss, crept back.

"Turned out to be no fizzle after all, for I found a miserable looking man lying on the ground, half starved, badly wounded in an arm, and looking like he'd been in the river that was close by.

"I reckoned he might be one of the crowd that worked with the Hawk—had an idea I'd seen him before in bad company; but he was a tough looking sight, and I just felt sorry for the bloke. So I fed him, and looked after his hurts, what with a heap of bruises, and a bullet through the fleshy part of his left arm.

"Then I got him on my mount, and carried him all the way to the station. The colonel took charge, and had him put to bed, with Doc. Hamilton looking after his troubles. He got better right away, and on the third day said he must be going. Then he confessed he had been a member of that Hawk gang and that his name was Gene Hotchkiss, though we both reckoned it was one he'd tacked on when he came up here to keep out of jail.

"He went on to tell us that he'd been fool enough to defy the Hawk when full of hard stuff; and how the other had flashed a gun to shoot him through the shoulder; then knocked him down, kicked him in a passion; and finally, when he was mighty near senseless, ordered two of his men to pick him up and throw him over a cliff into the river.

"How he managed to keep from being drowned when so weak and sore he couldn't explain—all he remembered was managing to pull himself out of the water when an eddy drew him in close to a shelving rock. Later on he tried to make his way along in the direction of Frazer's post, meaning to get out of this country, for his life would not be worth a pinch of salt if ever the Hawk learned he hadn't been put out of the way.

"He claimed to have a brother down in Winnipeg, and swore black and blue he was going back to him, so as to try and redeem himself. Colonel Astor encouraged him, feeling that what he spoke was the truth. Well, before he pulled out, going in company with a trapper chancing along right then, the chap was so grateful for all we'd done for him he up and told us a few things about the Hawk, such as we'd been crazy to learn for seven coons' ages.

"He described the location of the secret haunt of the gang, so we couldn't miss finding it when ready to pounce down on them. More than that he drew a sort of diagram, or chart, showing us how there was a back-door way of gettin' in, case they barricaded the main entrance—so far as he knew not a single guy of all the pack knew about this same rear door except himself; and he'd only found it out by sheer accident, keeping quiet, since he even then had a sneaking notion he'd have to pull out on the sly, if ever it came to a show-down between himself and the Hawk."

"That sounds like something well worth while," Jack remarked, after Red had apparently reached the end of his little yarn; "always provided what he told you was the truth, and not a fairy story invented to hoodwink you until he got out of touch, and could make his get-away."

"I believe it was backed by solid truth," Red stoutly affirmed; "and the colonel was of the same opinion. We were only waiting until several of the boys returned to the station after having their vacations, when we figured on pulling the roost, and closing out the whole bunch. Then you hit our place, and he made up his mind to let you have your day, backing you up when the posse arrived after their wild goose chase, sent on a false information that the gang planned to raid the little settlement at Frog's Neck down the river fifty miles or so."

Acting on Jack's request, Red explained (by means of the rude chart made by the so-called Gene Hotchkiss) just where the retreat was located; and also what course they would have to pursue if necessity compelled them to attempt to break in through the back door.

"If that stacks up against us," Jack finally decided, "we can go over this thing again and get our bearings—it may not be necessary if we have a decent share of luck. And now, boys, let's move along, and start something."

"When we get to a certain point," further advised the Mounty guide, "it's going to be necessary for us to leave the trail, hide our hosses, and take to the rocks."

"You reckon then they'll have a lookout posted to command the approach, and get wind of any threatening danger?" Jack asked.

"That Hotchkiss guy told us they never left anything to chance," Red explained; "he said that day and night a vidette is kept posted on a lookout point, where, unseen himself he can discover if even a fox comes along the only approach to the cave. He even said they had dynamite planted, with a wire running up to the den, so the whole works could be knocked into flinders if so be the Mounties came along. We've got to find that wire, and disconnect it first thing we do."

"Je-ru-sa-lem crickets! I should say so!" Perk chattered; "I ain't so set on doin' my flyin' in pieces that I'll cotton to any dynamite cache."

Then, as they were once more compelled to go single file on account of the rocks narrowing the trail, the consultation came to an end, and they continued to move ahead in utter silence save when a hoof chanced to strike the solid rock and made a subdued sound. Each rider, however, tried to keep this from happening whenever possible, by skillful guidance wth the bridle.

Perk kept watching the mountain that reared up its lofty peak thousands of feet above. It might be he was wondering what would happen should the guide through some mistake overlap the range of safety, and their coming be noted by the ever vigilant vidette posted in some eagle-like eyrie far up the slope.

Would their first warning of this fact be when a frightful explosion rent the atmosphere, and the massive rocks went flying in every direction, carrying themselves and their unlucky mounts along in sections? It was not a very cheerful subject to entertain, and Perk might be pardoned for feeling a little cold chill creep up and down his spinal column, when for instance he suddenly caught a rumbling sound, like an earthquake in its first throes. It however turned out to be simply a land-slide, such as frequently took place, as Perk himself very well knew, with great rocks, and a shower of loosened earth slipping down the slope with increasing momentum.

"Gosh a mity! that one near got my goat!" Perk told himself, with a nervous little laugh; and as he brought up the rear just then neither of his mates saw his brief spasm of alarm, for which he was thankful.

Suddenly Red threw up his arm. They had for some little time been walking their horses, and this warning signal brought them all to a complete standstill. Jack shoved up alongside the leader, and they exchanged looks.

"Here's where we got to leave our mounts, and go on afoot," was what Red explained, speaking in a low tone that added to the thrill of the occasion, at least so far as Perk was concerned. "See this red-looking rock that cuts out halfway across the trail—that Hotchkiss critter warned me not to pass it by—if we rode fifty feet further we'd come in line with the sentry up yonder."

"I guess now an inch is as good as a mile," Perk observed, grinning as though he had uttered some "wise crack" that did his discretion credit.

Looking around they soon found an opening in the wall on their right, through which the horses could be led. Red was particular to take the animals quite some distance away, so that in case one of them took a notion to neigh, as horses are apt to do at unexpected times, the sound might not be heard by the man on the lookout post, or by any one chancing to be passing along the trail.

So far so good; and yet the extra hazardous part of the undertaking was but beginning to loom up ahead.

CHAPTER XXIX

THE HAWK AT BAY

Red led the way, of course. Jack knew he was searching for the wire that ran from the planted explosive up to the spot where the vidette was stationed, his intention being to sever this strand so as to make the hidden dynamite futile for doing any damage.

Shortly afterwards the guide uttered a low exclamation as of satisfaction, following this up by kneeling down, and with a pair of pocket pliers cutting a wire that lay in plain sight on the rock.

Perk made a queer little noise, as though something in the way of a load had been taken from his chest. Jack, too, felt relieved; and besides, their early success seemed to presage a good ending to the adventure.

Again they went on, climbing by devious ways, but always making progress up toward the little plateau which had been described to Red by the former member of the bandit circle as the lookout's station.

Drawing gradually closer and closer in the

end they could make out the figure of a man, seated Arab fashion, with his legs drawn up under him, and watching the spot where the trail stood out so plainly to one far above. Apparently he had as yet discovered no suspicious movement, and was unaware of what virtually hovered over his own devoted head.

Again did Red assume the initiative, and Jack was perfectly willing that this should be his part. Whispering a few words in Jack's ear placed close to his lips, the Mounty sergeant moved away as noiselessly as a crawling serpent might have done, vanishing from their anxious eyes as though the rocks had opened to engulf him.

The two sky pilgrims crouched there and waited, keyed up to a high pitch of anticipation and excitement. Jack could hear Perk drawing in each breath with a slight rasping sound; so, too, did the other move restlessly as the minutes passed until a quarter of an hour had slipped by.

Then Jack noticed a faint movement just back of the lounging sentry, and something like four feet above his head. Of course it was Red, who had managed to attain this commanding spot without making any sound calculated to put the bandit lookout on the alert.

Perk, too, had glimpsed a face peering forth, and he as well as Jack suspended breathing as they saw the sturdy Mounty launch his body into space. Following came a scuffling noise, as the two forms writhed and twisted there on the out-cropping of rock, with a sheer drop of full a hundred feet, if one or both were so unfortunate as to squirm over the edge.

At least there had not been the faintest shout given, proving how perfect all of Red's movements had been calculated and carried out. No doubt the fingers of his right hand had clutched the sentry's throat in a flash, cutting off his wind, and reducing him to a condition of helplessness.

Two minutes afterwards and there was Red grinning as he beckoned for his two mates to climb up to where he awaited them. Upon reaching his side they found he had tied the prisoner's arms together behind his back; and Perk making a quick examination, nodded as if vastly pleased over such a thorough job. Borrowing a red bandana handkerchief—a fresh and new one Perk had laid in for this especial occasion—Red speedily made an effective gag which he secured over the senseless man's mouth, so that no matter how much he strove to cry out the best he could do would be to make a low moaning sound, hardly more than a grunt.

After this had been accomplished Red unceremoniously dragged him into an inviting fissure near by, where he could be left to himself. He had been coming into his senses at the time, and must have glimpsed the hated and feared uniform of the Mounties, which would be apt to give him a nightmare, knowing as he did what measure in the way of penalties was due for his reckoning.

Again the daring trio set out to reach the hidden den. Red led them by devious ways, always with the one thought of "playing safe" held up before him. Inside of five minutes he pointed to where a network of vines covered the face of a small cliff. Behind that curtain Red knew the secret entrance of the freebooters' rendezvous was to be found.

Red's hunch turned out to be all to the good, as was proven when they investigated, and found an opening that seemed to lead into the solid rock. Before taking chances by pushing into the black depths Jack and Red consulted once more in whispers.

Perk, hovering near by, suddenly glimpsed a moving object that turned out to be a hostile eavesdropper—undoubtedly one of the outlaws had been in the act of stepping out of the underground retreat when he made the thrilling discovery that the dreaded Mounties were at the door.

Knowing from Perk's actions that his presence was discovered, in a near panic the man attempted to get away. Perk, however, hoping to prevent Jack's plans for surprising the gang from being upset, made a furious rush toward the disappearing party.

He hurled himself upon the man, and succeeded in throwing him down with such violence that the other was knocked senseless; but unfortunately before this happened the outlaw had let out a warning shriek, that must have echoed through the passages of the cavern.

Several shots rang out, proving how quickly the gang could take the alarm. Loud voices, too, followed, and one in particular struck Jack as most dominant and commanding; so that it hardly needed the quick explanation from Red to tell Jack he was listening to the Hawk in person.

Perk, realizing that the battle was now on, started to do his share of the action; and the way he handled that machine-gun was a caution. Its rap-rap-rap following each burst with others in rapid succession, made it appear as though a dozen of the surprise party must be thronging at the entrance, ready for a concerted rush.

Perhaps, too, those sheltered inside the dark interior of the wonderful cavern could catch occasional glimpses of the hated and feared uniform of the Mounted Police; for Red was actively moving back and forth, with just this idea influencing him, to make them believe the entire force connected with the station had come upon the ground, bent upon making a complete sweep-up of the bunch at bay while they were about it.

The fight went on quite merrily for some little time, with shots echoing through the corridors of the underground retreat. Whether their hot fusilade was doing any harm the trio on the outside could not discover, for no longer were shouts being exchanged—the besieged bandits kept firing sullenly, nor did they seem to be lacking in an abundance of ammunition.

Realizing that they were getting nowhere by these ineffective tactics Jack again sought suggestions from his second in command. When Red vigorously advised that they try to find the secret rear entrance to the cavern, it struck Jack as a sensible plan. Knowing that there was little risk of the inmates making any serious attempt to rush out at this early stage of the battle, especially when unaware of the number of their foes, Jack concluded to accept the risks and take his whole inadequate force with him in making an attack from the rear.

It was indeed a lucky thing they had such a good guide at their disposal as Red proved to be; for he had no particular trouble in leading them along a narrow ledge, and through a branch of the main canyon, until they presently reached a dark crevice in the shape of a rock fault, exactly as his informant had advised would be the case.

This being the case they entered the split in the wall, and aided by occasional flashes from the hand electric torch Jack carried, managed in the end to reach the main cavern. Here torches fastened to the walls in the regulation fashion, allowed them to see the flitting figures of the alarmed bandits moving to and fro, as though engaged in changing their stores to some more secure location.

It appearing that only by a sudden rush could they hope to strike consternation into the hearts of the already panicky bunch, Jack gave the word, and with loud shouts and much firing of guns the three boldly rushed the enemy. In return came a volley of answering shots; but apparently this unexpected attack from the rear unnerved the outlaws, for breaking they rushed into an inner chamber, which had evidently been prepared for a last stand in case of just such an emergency as had now arrived. When the three came on the spot it was to find only a single form stretched on the rocky floor, and with a stout oaken door checking their further advance.

CHAPTER XXX

BACK OVER THE BORDER—CONCLUSION

Taking stock of the situation Jack found that things did not look so satisfactory as he could have wished. The outlaws, with but two missing from their number, so far as Jack could tell, had now retreated back of what seemed in the nature of a fort, which might defy all the efforts of himself and two companions to break in.

The thing that worried Jack most of all was the fact that Perk had been wounded in the last exchange of fierce firing. Just how serious this might prove he could not say; but his chum's left arm seemed to hang helplessly at his side; although otherwise the war veteran displayed his usual scorn of a little blood-letting on his part.

"Looks kinder like we might be up a tree, partner," Perk hoarsely told him as they came together while dodging the hot firing. "Mebbe now you'd better gimme permission to heave a couple o' them little tear gas marbles into that ere hole in the wall! See there's a place right over that same heavy door they left open for ventilation like; I could make a little rush up and

245

push the pills through it in three shakes o' a
lamb's tail. Say the word, buddy, an' let's end
all this guess work."

Jack himself realized it would be their best
policy; he had before then witnessed the effective nature of those same small bombs under conditions not so very unlike those now confronting
them; and remembered how mutinies in jails and
penitentiaries down in the States were being effectually quelled by the use of similar methods.

"All right, Perk, have your way; the quicker
it's done the better, for I must have a look at
that arm of yours, old man."

Perk seemed well pleased, and lost not a second in "getting a move on," as he himself would
have termed it. Making a speedy dash he managed to reach the vicinity of the fastened door,
drew back his right arm, and then shot it forward. A second time was the movement carried
out, after which he staggered along the rocky
wall, and fell at Jack's feet as if exhausted by
his supreme effort.

Jack's first impulse was to bend down in order
to see what he could do to help his wounded pal;
but Perk refused to be counted out.

"Go on and play the game to a finish, buddy,"
snapped the other, managing to attain a sitting
posture, and pawing for his gun, lying close by;
"I'm all to the good—don't bother 'bout me

now—get your men first thing—I'll hold out
okay—go to it, partner. Gosh! jest hear 'em
whoopin' things up, will you?"

The inmates of the barricaded fort were indeed creating a frightful row, cursing, and shouting, and begging some one to open the door so as
to give them fresh air, saying their eyesight was
gone, and they were stone blind.

Red had taken up his position close to one side
of the door, as if waiting to nail the first fellow
who came staggering forth, groping in utter
darkness, and with his eyeballs smarting fright-
fully; so there was nothing for Jack to do but
back the efficient Mounty up.

One of the prisoners and victims of the tear
gas bombs managed to remove the bar holding
the massive door; and as they came staggering
forth, one after another, those awaiting seized
hold, frisked them for weapons, and with in-
credible swiftness snapped a pair of handy steel
bracelets upon their several wrists.

It was soon all over but the shouting—there
proved to be six of the outlaws, including the
Hawk himself. The latter, when undergoing
the agonies attending the effects of the gas, displayed no symptoms of his accustomed bravado,
although he did not whimper, and plead, like
some of the other victims.

Jack hastened to take a look at Perk's wound,

and found that while he had lost considerable blood, and seemed weak, there was not anything very serious about it—a rest of several days would set him on his feet again without any doubt.

Anxious to get back to the station with their prisoners they lost no time in looking over the secret hiding place of the now demoralized gang which could wait for another day; but loading the prisoners on the horses, made a speedy start. Three hours later what was their delight to suddenly meet a body of Mounties heading toward the scene of the recent battle; and at their head rode none other than Colonel Ascot himself.

As Dr. Hamilton was believed to be at the trading post, and Jack wished to have him look after Perk, they headed in that direction first of all, each of the troopers having one of the dejected prisoners in front of him astride his mount.

Their coming created quite a sensation at the post, and the old factor quite naturally rejoiced at the prospect of presently recovering all the stock so recently carried off by the bold swoop of the outlaw gang. Since the leading spirit of the organization, known to them only as the Hawk, was booked to be returned to Leavenworth; and the minor offenders would get their liberty cut off for years to come, it looked as though peace was likely to reign throughout that section of the Northwest Territory for keeps.

After Perk's arm had been cared for it was determined to keep on in the direction of the Mounties' headquarters, carrying all their prisoners along. They reached their objective about noon on the following day, not being able to make fast progress on account of the double burdens carried by the horses.

Then came the biggest surprise of all, so far as Jack and Perk were concerned. The former and Dr. Hamilton were having a little chat, and Perk on his part sat in the sun amusing himself by staring at something he held in his one good hand. Jack, as if by accident, steered his companion over that way, so they came up behind Perk, quite unaware of their presence. He was, as might be said to be his habit, talking with himself.

"Hang the luck!" they heard him mutter as if greatly annoyed; "there she slipped me again, jest like the greased pig they try to ketch in that silly game—I was goin' to say that name as slick as you please, but now I lost connections again. Adrian—Adrian *what*?"

"Where did you get that picture?" demanded a voice close to his ear, as a hand shot out and snatched it from his grasp.

"Why—what—here, what business you got takin' my property?" gasped Perk as turning his

head awkwardly he looked in astonishment at
Dr. Hamilton, strangely excited; while Jack
stood by, nodding his head, and grinning, as if
some suspicion he had entertained was now con-
firmed.

"Because he is *my* boy—I am Doctor Adrian
Bahrman!"

When the surgeon said this as though determined to no longer hide his identity behind a
false name, Perk gave a tremendous start, and
turning to Jack cried out:

"Hot diggetty dig! *did* you hear that, partner—he said it, the name I been tryin' to get out
for ever so long! Knowed it was somethin' that
begun with a B, didn't I tell you? Now I c'n
get some peace, anyway. An' me always won-
derin' where I'd seen a face like you'rn, Doc.
Shake hands on that."

Of course Jack had to tell the story, and when
the thrilled doctor learned how Perk had evidently saved the lives of his dear ones he again
wrung the unbandaged hand of that individual
with might and main, tears streaming down his
cheeks.

They had decided to spend several more days
at the station, so Perk would be in condition for
the return trip; and there were frequent occasions for the whole story to be told on both sides.

Dr. Bahrman told them just why he had been
influenced to hide himself away up in the wilderness—he had been betrayed by a cousin of his
wife's, who had once been a suitor for her hand
in marriage. So cleverly had a plot been woven
around him that through circumstantial evidence
it seemed as though he were guilty of a forgery,
and when out on bail he had been urged to flee,
especially by his wife.

When he learned how Adrian's mother was
now searching for him, with good news of some
sort, he decided to go back to the States with
Jack, and take his chances of being freed from
the odium of being a fugitive from justice.

But just the same a turn of Fortune's wheel
decided that this should not be—that having suffered for all these months from the outrageous
flings of malice and hatred, things had suddenly
changed for the better.

On the day before the one selected for making
a start in the airship, carrying their moody cap-
tive with them, there was a sudden burst of shouting; and as Jack hurried out of the log building
he was thrilled to catch the strangely familiar
throbbing sound of a plane in the heavens. They
stood there, every one at the station, watching the
oncoming of a sky-racer; and even before it
dropped down Perk had pronounced it a new-
model Sikorsky Amphibian, Wasp powered, he

being more or less of an authority on such matters.

But as it turned out that was only a small part
of the surprise awaiting them; for no sooner had
the boat settled in the river close to shore than
two men landed, helping a woman and a child
along. Jack saw Dr. Bahrman start to run toward them as fast as his legs could carry him;
and just as he was suspecting would prove to be
the case, when the woman hurriedly snatched off
the goggles and helmet she had been wearing, he
recognized her as the mother of little Adrian,
quickly to be wrapped in the arms of her eager
husband; nor did the dancing boy have to wait
long ere he too was held in a close embrace.

The story Mrs. Bahrman told was like a leaf
taken from some volume of fairy tales. The
wicked cousin had been overtaken by the penalty
for his plotting, having been in a serious road accident when his car was smashed by a train at a
crossing; but before he died he had the decency
to make a sworn statement before a justice of the
peace, entirely exonerating Dr. Bahrman from
the forgery charge that had been skillfully woven
around him, so that nothing now stood in the way
of the reunited family returning to their former
home, and taking up their lives just where this
wretched happening separated them.

Mrs. Bahrman, remembering that she had a

brother in the Navy who was an efficient aviator and had made quite a name for himself, sought his assistance the very day after she and her boy had been saved from the burning tenement in Salt Lake City, he being stationed in Los Angeles at the time.

This brother being in high favor with the authorities readily secured permission to use a new Government ship just placed in his charge; and carrying an assistant pilot, along with the two Bahrmans, start over the line for Canada, the devoted wife having in some way learned that her absent mate might be found in the vicinity of the advanced northern frontier post of the Mounties.

So after all, when Jack and Perk started on the following day, it was with the knowledge that soon afterwards the Sikorsky would be following them, carrying a happy party homeward bound.

They had no trouble with their prisoner, who seemed to be of a reckless disposition, and snapping his fingers at Fate—he only said he had had a run for his money, and could afford to let matters take their course—that a man could die but once, and after all they did not treat prisoners badly at Fort Leavenworth.

Having duly delivered their man to the Federal District Attorney in Spokane who would see that he was returned to the penitentiary, Jack and Perk again waited further orders from Washington that would send them forth upon yet another flight through the clouds, following the path of duty.

THE END